TWISTED ROOTS

Vanessa Johnson

ISBN-13: 9798649923187

Cover design by: Logan Hawkins
Library of Congress
Control Number: 2018675309
Printed in the United States of America

For Felicity, Dax and Brynn

PROLOGUE

It was late December, close to Christmas time. Christmas was supposed to be full of joy, hope and family. For her it was a time of pain, resentment and bitterness. There was nothing to look forward to anymore. It had been years since she had heard from any of her family. It was just her, all alone on Christmas, and she was used to it.

Her apartment was bare and undecorated. She stared out the window of her one-bedroom apartment and watched the snow fall lightly on the street below. It looked sterile and untouched outside. She remembered an earlier time when she had loved the snow – even thought it was beautiful. It was just starting to get dark outside, but the bright Christmas lights seemed to make the whole city glow.

A knock at the door startled her. She wasn't expecting company. She walked across the cushy carpet to her front door and cautiously opened it. Her eyes widened as she stared at the young woman standing before her. She hadn't seen her sister in almost two years. Last she'd heard, she had gone off to attend some prestigious university and hadn't bothered to call. They had always been so close and the separation had wounded her deeply.

"What do you want?" she asked her. She stared at the woman who had been such a huge part of her. It had been so long that being so close to her felt like tiny little pins were poking into her heart at lightening speed. Second by second she could feel her chest tightening, she was going to fall apart.

"I – I need your help." Her sister's voice quivered, and her whole body shook. She held her arms out and began to cry.

The sister on the receiving end stared at the bundle in front of her. A baby. A beautiful baby girl, wrapped up so tightly you could barely see her. She stared blankly at her sister. This wasn't the woman she knew, the girl she had grown up with. This woman in front of her was timid and afraid, more like a baby herself.

"I need you to keep her," her sister said, carefully holding out the baby. "I – I need to go get some help for a while. She'll be better off with you."

"What? You can't just give me your baby." The woman was confused and surprised.

"Please. She's better off with you." She pushed the baby into her arms and whispered her name to her sister. It was a beautiful name – pure, like a snow-covered Christmas morning. *"I'll be in touch."* She pulled out a diaper bag from behind her and put it on the floor. Then in a split second, she turned and ran down the hallway so fast she didn't even hear the voice of her sister calling after her.

The woman looked down at the little baby in her arms. She was frozen. She didn't know how to react. A beautiful baby girl smiled up at her and made a soft cooing noise.

"Well, baby," she said. *"Looks like it's just you and me."* She began to rock her slowly and carefully in her arms, taking her into the apartment and shutting the door behind them.

ONE
Kate

For as long as I can remember, morning has always been my favourite time of day. There is something so tranquil about the morning and the peace that it holds. Everything is fresh and quiet, and the stillness that surrounds it seems to take on new possibilities. I find joy in being awake before the rest of the world and checking things off my list as soon as possible. I'm also a list person. My mother used to tell me that I'd made lists for my lists from the moment I'd learned how to use a pencil.

Fife Springs is quiet in the morning, and each day my morning begins with a 5am run through the quaint, petite town. I run a steady three to five miles before retreating home and taking a long, rejuvenating shower. Afterwards, I sit in my kitchen with my iPad, reading the paper and sipping on coffee until the town begins to stir. The morning is usually the only time I have to myself – that is until, I have to drag my teenage daughter by her claws out of her bedroom.

My job is very high profile in our little town. I'm judge, one of two judges to be precise, and the only one whom is female and also the younger of the two. Because of this, all eyes are always on me anywhere and everywhere I go. This typically means that I don't get very much alone time, another reason why I take advantage of my early mornings.

I stretch my toes out on the bottom of the barstool beside me, and then take a large sip of coffee. Coffee is my saving grace for many reasons. Firstly, it allows me to function off of limited sleep. Secondly, it wards off numerous headaches from daily encounters with civilians who think I owe them numerous legal favours. And thirdly, it gives me enough patience to deal with my daughter Holly, who lately has been acting like I've married and sold my soul to Satan himself.

I look towards the digital stove clock, and I see the time switch to 7:30am. I close my eyes and brace myself, knowing that my morning silence will be over in a matter of seconds. I listen carefully but hear no movement coming from upstairs. I put down my coffee mug and sigh, walking out of the kitchen and up the stairs, mentally preparing myself for another battle.

TWO
Holly

"Holly. Holly!" My mom bursts through my bedroom door and my eyes shoot open like cannons. "You're going to be late."

Rolling over in my bed, I groan in reply. "Ten more minutes," I mumble, stretching out my legs beneath the soft cotton sheets.

"Holly," my mom's too-slim figure shadows over me. "I'm due in court in an hour. I'm going to be late. If you want a ride -."

"I'll walk," I cut her off and bury my face in my pillow. Turning my head to the side I call out, "Maybe if you'd let me get my license I could drive myself."

"You just turned sixteen."

I can picture her shaking her head at me.

"It's the middle of winter," she goes on. "You can get your license in the spring when the roads are better. Every month I see so many young people in my court room who -."

"I know, I know," I cut her off again. "Have lost their lives…such a tragedy."

My mom sighs, less than impressed with my attitude. "I'm going to go start breakfast. You have ten minutes." She exits my bedroom, and I dramatically throw my face back down onto my pillow.

I grudgingly pull myself out of bed, and I put on the first clean clothes that I can find. I walk down the hall into the bathroom, and I check out my appearance in the mirror. I grab a can of hair mousse off the counter and dispense some into my hand. Rubbing my palms together I run it through my blonde curly hair, adding some bounce to it. I quickly coat my lashes with a thin layer of mascara and rub some Chapstick over my lips with my index finger.

Taking the stairs two at a time, I walk straight into the kitchen. Our kitchen looks like a kitchen you would see on an HGTV show after the renovation has been completed. It's full on stainless steel appliances, along with light oak cabinets and counters so clean one could perform surgery on them. Everything has a place, and my mom's system of order screams perfection at all times.

I reach for a mug, pour myself a cup of coffee and sit down on a bar stool at the island. My mom sits beside me at the shiny granite counter top reading through a stack of papers, sipping a mug of coffee, as well as watching the eggs frying on the stove all at the same time. A small part of me secretly hopes that she burns the eggs.

Kate Sherwood is a machine. She is well-oiled with all of her parts in mint condition. Her exterior is glowing and solid. Her ivory skin has tones of bubble gum pink. She is opposite to me in appearance with her shoulder length dark brown hair and her light brown eyes. Her cheekbones are well defined and her jaw forms a perfect U shape. She is easily one of the most beautiful women I have ever seen. She holds herself in a way that is so flawless that it seems effortless to everyone around her. She is always proper, well-behaved and seems to have time for everyone in the world, except for maybe me. She works a lot. She is a courtroom judge, and she is very busy. Because of this, I don't see her much during the week as she's always working late or at meetings. Whenever we are out in public it feels like I need to compete with half the town to get my own mom's attention.

Being a junior in high school and having a mother who is a public figure doesn't go hand in hand. My mom has the impressive life skill of knowing everything I do the moment that it happens. If I so much as even hold a drink that isn't punch at party, she knows. If I act out in public, am late to school, or heaven forbid cut a class, she knows. Although I never know how she finds out these things, Mom claims she has spies everywhere. She's strict, but she's also fair – as fair as parents go, I guess.

Mom places a plate of eggs in front of me. "Eat," she tells me, and holds out a fork. I take the fork from her and slowly begin to pick at the eggs. "Do you want a ride?"

"If you can't that's okay." I put a small piece of egg into my mouth. The phone rings.

"Hello?" Mom answers it on the second ring, without even looking at the screen. "Oh, hi Gwen." Gwen Sherwood is my aunt, and Mom's twin sister. "Yes, tonight. I'll be pretty late. That would be great. Hold on, I'll ask her." She holds the phone away from her ear and looks over at me. "Sweetheart, Gwen wants to know if you want her to pick you up from school. She's going to come have dinner with you tonight; I have a big meeting and will be gone most of the night."

"I don't need a babysitter." I scowl and push the practically untouched plate of eggs back towards Mom. She always had a big meeting. "And I'm not hungry."

"Did you hear that Gwen?" Mom sighs. "Okay." She holds out the phone to me. "She wants to talk to you." I take the phone.

"Hi," I grumble.

"Hey love," Gwen's gentle voice greets me. "So it's a slow day at the clinic and I get to close early, so I was telling your mom that I wanted to do some shopping and could really use a young, hip opinion." I can practically hear her smiling through the phone. "So I was thinking I'd pick you up after school and then we'd head down to Sally's and get some pedicures. After that we can hit up a few stores, shop for a bit and then grab dinner. Your pick, my treat; what do you say?"

Gwen is a doctor. She shares a practice in town with Dr. Andrew Daniels, who is a younger male doctor. Next to my mother, Gwen was the closest thing I had to a second parental figure while growing up. My father had been out of the picture since the day I was born. My mom refuses to talk about him; I don't even know his name. This used to bother me a lot, but over the years I've just gotten used to the fact that Mom is a closed book when it comes to him. I've tried to find out information about my father for years, but Mom hasn't even offered up a picture.

Aunt Gwen is what I like to call, "the cool aunt that every teenage girl needs." The aunt who you can call in the middle of the night to come get you, who will spoil you rotten and who you can confide in about everything, knowing they won't rat you out to your mother. Well, maybe that last part isn't true. Gwen tells my mom everything, but there's some unwritten code that when she does, Mom doesn't bring it up.

"Yeah," I say into the phone, "I guess that would be alright."

"Great," Gwen exclaims. "I'll see you later then. Okay, sweetie?"

"Sure."

"I love you."

"You too. You want to talk to Mom again?"

"Tell her I'll call her later."

I hang up the phone. "She said she'll call you later."

"I can drive you if we leave now," Mom offers.

"Sure." I stand up from her chair.

"Aren't you going to finish your eggs?" She furrows her eyebrows and purses her lips, showing a look of concern.

"You just said…"

"Okay, okay," she says, holding up her hands defensively "Let's go." Mom straightens out her black pencil skirt and black suit jacket. As always, she manages to look elegant and classy, like she has just stepped out of a magazine page.

I, on the other hand, am another story. Wearing a pair of ripped jeans, black Converse sneakers and a white wrinkled t-shirt with "LOVE" scrawled across the front in black writing, I look a little rough around the edges, as Mom likes to call it. My blonde curls are already beginning to fall wildly around my face; we've always had trouble taming my mane of hair.

I stare at myself in the floor-length mirror that covers our hall closet. I note the bags under my eyes. I look tired, like I haven't slept in days. I sigh and turn to look at Mom who is standing there watching me. I narrow my eyes at her, and she continues to stare, not acknowledging that I'm now facing her.

"Are we going to go?" I roll my eyes. "Or are you just going to stand there and stare at me all day?"

"Have you lost weight?" My mom scrunches her eyes at me, giving me a once over.

"Doubtful," I snort in reply.

"You didn't even touch your breakfast."

"I don't feel well." I shrug. This is half true. My heart is racing, my stomach feels like someone is kicking it on repeat and, more than anything, I want to halt this conversation.

Mom immediately walks over to me and puts her hand on my forehead. "You don't feel warm."

"Cramps."

"Ah. Do you need anything?"

"I thought you were going to be late." I motion towards the door.

"You need a jacket," she points out. She's not wrong. It's the middle of winter.

I groan. "Don't tell me you're going for mother of the year all of a sudden." Mom flinches in response; I can tell my words have hurt her. I don't know why I said that. Lately things have been tense between us. Mom walks towards the front door and opens the entry closet. She hands me my black leather jacket and puts on her sleek black trench coat.

"Let's go." Mom holds open the front door and I follow her outside. We get into her black SUV and drive to school in silence.

We make it just in time, as the first bell is sounding. "I'm in court most of the day," Mom tells me. "So if you need anything –."

"I'll call the courthouse because you won't have your phone. I know the drill."

Mom reaches out to push a strand of my hair behind my ear.

"Are you sure you're okay?" she asks.

"Never been better." I give her an over-the-top smile. "Thanks for the ride."

"Okay, well I'll see you tonight?"

"Sure."

"Have fun with Gwen."

"Have fun at work." I open the door and climb out of the car.

"I love –." I hear Mom start to say it, but I slam the door shut before she can finish and begin the walk up towards the school.

THREE
Kate

I watch Holly walk towards the school, and I feel a familiar feeling of defeat weigh on my heart. I don't know why she dislikes me so much. I know that teenage girls and their mothers aren't supposed to get along; it's practically a rite of passage. Things used to be so much simpler. Growing up it was always just Holly and I against the world. I'd been a lawyer working at a small practice in a small town. I was busy but not too busy. We had moved to Fife Springs when Holly was seven years old. Before that I had been juggling work as a legal assistant, while working hard to graduate from law school.

About two years ago, I was encouraged to interview for the position of a second judge opening. I did so on a whim, knowing it would be a great career move, but also not expecting anything to come of it. I had been thirty-four years old at the time and knew that my chances were less than likely. Much to my surprise, I was offered the position and accepted it. I love my job, but I know that it has affected my relationship with my daughter in more ways than I am proud to admit.

I work long days. I'm constantly called into meetings and adding tasks to a list that never seems to end. I also bring my work home with me – a lot. You'd think that being a judge in a smaller town would have its perks. Typically speaking, small towns like Fife Springs aren't known for high crime rates. However, we also serve as the court for several other towns that reach our borders and cannot capacitate their own courthouse. So yes, this means my days are busy and full. It also means that Holly spends a lot of time with my twin sister Gwen. Gwen has her own medical practice, which means that while she works a lot, she does have some freedom with her schedule. She starts her days early and also ends them earlier than I can.

Holly sees Gwen as the "fun" aunt. I know it's good for them to spend time together, but part of me resents my sister for it. I wish for one day I didn't need to be seen as the hard-ass mom, but that I

could just take my daughter and have some fun with her. For a brief
moment, I wonder what that would be like. I could just abandon all
of my responsibilities, grab Holly and we could go spend the day
somewhere. Holly would probably think that I was having a stroke. I
sigh, and continue my drive to the courthouse.

I pull into my official parking spot that read "Reserved for
The Honourable K. Sherwood." Usually even on the worst days, just
seeing that sign can bring a smile to my face. I've accomplished a lot
for being a single mom with not a lot of resources. I'd raised Holly
by myself from the beginning. Mine and Gwen's parents had passed
away in a car accident when we were eighteen and we didn't have
any other family. It had always just been Holly and I. Gwen had
moved back to town after her residency was finished when Holly
was around eight years old. Holly had been infatuated with Gwen
since the day they had met. She told me that Gwen looked like a
dolly – actually she looked exactly like Holly. No one could ever
question that they were related.

I gather my thoughts, pick my briefcase up off the floor and
get out of my vehicle. I walk from the parking lot around the
building to the front of the courthouse. Many eyes attempt to catch
mine as I pass them. I give a quick smile or a wave and keep
walking. If I stopped for every person who wanted to steal me for a
"quick second," I would never get inside.

I enter into the courthouse and quickly get waved through by
security. I've almost made it to my chambers when a voice calls out,
"Aren't you forgetting something?" I try to catch myself, but I smile.
I turn around and see a familiar face walking towards me.

Duane Edison is the head detective in town. We'd met years
ago when I had first moved to Fife Springs. Me, the aspiring lawyer,
fresh out of law school and him a rookie police officer learning the
ropes of a small town. Duane smiles as he walks up to me and hands
me a coffee. "Just the way you like it," he says.

"Bless your heart. I need this today." I smile again.

"Holly still being a pain-in-the-butt teenager again?" He
winks at me and his dark eyes sparkle. Duane looked like the kind of
detective you'd see in a made-for-TV movie. He was 6'2 with dark
brown eyes, dark chocolate brown hair and a light russet-brown skin
that looked like it belonged on a television commercial and a figure
that – well, let's just say it didn't hurt him one bit.

"Something like that," I frown.

"Meet me for lunch today?" Duane whispers.

"I should be able to make that work. Same place?"

"Always. Have a great day, Katie." He was the only person besides Gwen who called me that. He places his hand lightly on my arm and walks away. To anyone else it would have looked like a friendly gesture, but to me it was the world. Duane had been one of my only and best friends for the first few years we had lived here. We were both single, so it was easy enough for us to have a platonic relationship. Then suddenly it wasn't. I'll never forget the night that Duane had told me he loved me and wanted more. I'd tried to push him away, but it was undeniable.

So we'd started dating with a few unconventional terms. No one knew except for Gwen, not even Holly. With our professions it wasn't seen as suspicious for us to be seen together on numerous occasions that could be considered professional outings. Business lunches and dinners were very common for me. While Holly knew Duane and liked him, I just hadn't been ready for that yet. I knew that bringing Duane into our lives that way would bring up questions that I wasn't ready to answer. Questions that I didn't know how to answer. Holly had stopped asking about her father by the time she was six years old. Even as a young child she had become intuitive that I was a closed book on the subject, and had for the most part given up. Duane and I had been together for almost two years. I knew our relationship was getting to the point where he was wanting more. Every time he brought up marriage, I changed the subject. I knew deep down that I wouldn't be able to keep changing the subject for much longer.

FOUR
Holly

I walk into school, already counting the minutes until I get to leave. I hate school. It's full of snobs, stereotypes and unrealistic expectations. I'm not a nerd or anything like that, but I don't hang out with the popular crowd either. I'm what some would call a floater. Emma and I have been best friends since we met in elementary school and the two of us are inseparable. It's nice to have consistency in such an inconsistent place.

I approach my locker and mechanically turn the lock to open the door. Before looking inside, I turn to the left and see Griffin Anderson walking towards me. The butterflies in my stomach begin to flutter and I feel my body temperature start to rise. Griffin often had this effect on me. I take in his bronze-brown eyes, his short black curly hair and his deep caramel bronze skin and think my knees will buckle.

"Hey, Sherwood," he whispers into my ear. "We still on for tonight?" I wet my lips and nod. "Good, I'll text you later." He protectively puts a hand on my waist for a brief second – so brief that you'd miss it if you weren't paying attention – and continues walking down the hallway.

Griffin and I have had a "thing" for about a month now. Griffin Anderson is a star. He's captain of the soccer team and one of the most popular guys in school. One night at a party where Emma had ditched me for a basketball player, he'd driven me home and kissed me good night in the driveway.

From then on, he would pick me up almost every night after my mother had gone to bed. We'd fool around a little and then he would take me back home. Our relationship has also been a secret. I don't like labels, and Griffin isn't allowed to date during soccer season. Plus a public relationship with Griffin would be like dating the Prom King, and that just isn't my thing.

Last night we had been in the park together until 2am looking up at the stars, wrapped together in a blanket, when he had told me he loved me. I'd just kissed him in response. Love wasn't something

I was ready to explore yet. Sex on the other hand was another story. Lately Griffin had become more explorative with me when it came to our sexual relationship. His hands had started wandering in new places, and he wanted more.

If there was one thing I knew about sex it's that I needed to be prepared. If I was going to have sex with Griffin, I needed protection. Mom would kill me if I got pregnant - well honestly, my mother would probably kill me if she knew I was thinking about having sex to begin with. I'd been planning to go to the doctor during my spare period after lunch and find out more about birth control.

However, there's one slight problem with living in a small town. There's only one doctor's office and my aunt Gwen works there. Gwen usually starts her days early and is off by noon. My plan was to sneak in an appointment when my aunt is off and pray that she will never find out.

"Look alive, Holly." Emma's voice startles me.

"Hey," I clear my throat and reach into my locker for a textbook.

"What's up with you?"

"Not much." I find my math textbook and start searching for my calculator.

"You've been staring in your locker for a good five minutes."

"Can't find my calculator," I begin rummaging through my books. Where was it?

"What did Griffin want?" Emma's blue eyes graze over my face.

"What?" I stop looking and turn to face Emma.

"I saw Griffin talking to you…"

"Oh," I shake my head. "He just wanted to borrow my math notes."

"Ah. Have you seen Carter yet?" Carter is one of our friends. Sometimes I think Emma wishes that he could be more than that.

"Nope," I reach deep into my locker and feel around for the calculator. I finally find its square edge and pull it out.

"Oh." Emma shakes her long brown hair and tucks a few loose pieces behind her ear. Her already pink cheeks look extra flushed. I can tell she has more to say, but I'm too distracted to push it.

"Walk me to math?"

"Let's go."

I shut my locker door, link my arm through Emma's and together we walk down the school hallway. Emma lives a block away from us and over the years I've spent most days at Emma's house after school. Emma is one of five siblings and there is always something going on at her house.

"What are you doing tonight?" Emma asks. "Mom's making her pot roast. Want to come over?" Mrs. Field's cooking was to die for and her pot roast was my absolute favourite meal.

"Ah I wish," I shake my head. "Mom's working late so I'm hanging out with Gwen."

"Fun!" Emma grins. "Have you finally met her mystery man?" My aunt Gwen had begun dating a man named Chad several weeks earlier; unfortunately a name was all the info we had been able to get out of her.

"Nope." I make a face. "She won't tell me anything."

"I bet he's a dream boat."

"I sure hope he doesn't resemble any kind of boat…"

"Shut it!" Emma laughs. "Anyways I need to get to class. See you at lunch?"

"Ummm," I bite my lower lip. "Not today. I have to study…I'll be in the library."

"Lunch time is not for studying," Emma says firmly.

"Sorry girl, catch you later!" I wave at Emma and duck my head into my class, escaping any future conversation.

I'm hardly able to keep my head on my shoulders until lunchtime. I've felt nauseous and dizzy all morning. Focus is something that feels extremely far off. First I have math, followed by French – which was my least favourite subject, but Mom had insisted I take it.

When the bell finally rings for lunch, I sneak off campus as quickly as possible trying to remain unseen. Fife Springs is a small town. Almost everything is in walking distance, which means that you are always going to be seen by someone you know. For me this means that if the wrong person sees me going into the doctor's office, my mother will find out about it in a minute flat.

I pull the hood of my jacket up and walk the ten-minute walk with my head down. When I get to the parking lot I don't see Gwen's car, so I assume it is safe to assume that she has gone home for the day. I walk into the doctor's office with my head still down and walk up to the front receptionist desk.

"Holly!" Trudy, the receptionist greets me. "How are you, honey? Are you here to see Dr. Sherwood?"

"Hi Trudy," I keep my voice as low as I can. "No, I'm here to see Dr. Daniels." I name my aunt Gwen's co-practitioner. "If he has time."

"Oh, sure," Trudy smiles at me. She is a plump woman in her early sixties, with salt-and-pepper coloured hair, pasty white skin and a big smile that's always plastered on her face. "I can take you into a room right now if you want. It's slow today."

"Perfect." I watch as Trudy grabs my file from the massive wall-covering shelf behind her. She walks out from behind the desk area and opens the side door that links the waiting area to the hallway of examination rooms. I follow her down the hall and into a room. I sit down on a rock hard, burgundy-coloured chair and stare straight at the white wall.

"So honey, what brings you in today?"

I take a deep breath. I have prepared myself for this question. "It's personal," I say in a tone that I hope sounds confident.

Trudy raises her eyebrows at me and looks curious, "Okay." I can tell she thinks it's absolutely absurd that a sixteen-year-old would have anything "personal." She smiles anyway. "Dr. Daniels will be in to see you shortly."

I sit in the small, sterile, bare examination room waiting anxiously. About five minutes later, the door opens and my aunt Gwen walks in. I jump up from the chair I was sitting in, my eyes wide.

"Holly?" My aunt raises her eyebrows at me, a confused expression appearing on her face.

I'm instantly caught off guard. She isn't supposed to be here. So I say the first thing that comes to my mind. "You're not Dr. Daniels," I stammer.

An amused look crosses my aunt's face. "Not I'm not," she replies and winks at me.

I don't know what to say next. I try to think of a lie but nothing is coming to mind.

"Sit down," Gwen tells me. She shuts the door and sits down on the black swirly stool in front of the counter. I sit. "I walked past the door and saw your name on the file, so I asked Trudy if you were here. She wouldn't tell me why you were here, so I figured I would just ask you myself. So, why are you here? Are you sick?"

I link my fingers together, stretching my arms out in front of me. "No, I'm not sick."

"Then why are you at the doctors?" She asks this in a tone that tells me she thinks I'm being ridiculous.

"I just needed to talk to a doctor, and Dr. Daniel's is a doctor."

"I'm a doctor."

"You're my aunt; you aren't supposed to treat me. Isn't it unethical or something?"

Gwen sighs. She tucks a strand of stray hair behind her right ear and fidgets with the stethoscope around her neck before looking me directly in the eyes. "Holly, what's going on?"

I'm the spitting image of Gwen. It can almost be eerie at times. We have the same cheekbones, same jaw line and the same blonde mane of hair. Although, mine is longer and more unruly, while hers is kept shorter to her chin and her curls are neat and well maintained. Same yellow bronze-tanned skin and olive-green eyes, nothing like my mom's baby doll pink cheeks and brown eyes.

While growing up, people had always thought Gwen was my mom, and to be honest I'd wished it some of the time. Supposedly our genes took after my grandfather who had died before I was born. Gwen is my mother's twin after all, so it makes sense that there would be some resemblance between us. There is something about my aunt Gwen that is just so cool. She still acts young and she is always available, relatable and easy to talk to. She never seems too busy for me and will even drop work to be with me, something I can't even imagine my own mother doing.

"Don't be mad," I say.

"Always a good introduction," she shakes her head at me.

I close my eyes and wince, a painful expressing covering my face. "I want to know about birth control."

"Birth control," Gwen says the words slowly and drags them out. Her facial expression remains intact and I can't tell what she's thinking. "Holly, does your mom know you're here?"

"Legally I don't need my mother here to get a birth control prescription," I point out. "I'm over sixteen."

"True, but you're still a minor." Gwen taps her index finger against her temple. "Okay then. Are you sexually active?" I hesitate. I can feel my face turning a dark shade of purple. The room suddenly feels like I'm sitting in a sauna. Gwen's tone softens. "Holly, I ask these questions to everyone. It's my job."

I nod. "No, I haven't done it yet." I notice her start to make a face at my use of the word "it" and then catch herself.

"Are you planning on being sexually active with more than one partner?"

"At a time?" I make a face that shows how horrifying her suggestion is to me.

"Yes."

"No way."

She goes on to describe how after I become sexually active I will need to come in for a PAP smear and regular checkup. She talks about safe sex and finding out my partner's sexual history. Finally she takes out her prescription pad. "I'm starting you on a low dosage of birth control. Remember, it can take up to a full month for the pill to be effective so if you are planning on being sexually active before then, be sure to use a secondary form of protection."

I have to hand it to the woman; she's playing it very cool. She goes on to describe some common side effects of the pill she's giving me, as well as how I should take it. When we both stand up to leave, I say, "I thought you'd be mad and give me some lecture on how I'm too young to be sexually active."

My aunt smiles at me. "As your doctor I'm not of liberty to do that. As your aunt, however, let's just say it's going to be a long night." That wipes the smile off my face. "I'll see you at 3pm outside the school. Don't be late."

"Fine, bye." I turn to walk out of the room.

"Hey!" She calls out. I turn around and give her a questioning look. "Don't I even get a hug from my favourite niece?" I roll my eyes in response but walk over and give her a quick hug. I start to pull away but she squeezes me tight. "I love you, Holly. Be careful, okay?"

I ignore her last comment. "I love you too, and I have to get back for English. I'll see you later."

Gwen holds her left arm up in a wave and I walk out of her office. I get outside and the cold January air hits me; I realize that my heart is still racing and my face feels like it's on fire. I wipe my sweaty palms on my jeans and walk over to the pharmacy instead of going back to school.

I drop my prescription off, trying to avoid the hawk eyes of the town I can feel following my every move. I wait for fifteen minutes, hiding behind a magazine stand, and then pick up my prescription. I'm heading out of the pharmacy when I look to my left and see Mom walking out of the courthouse right across the street.

My stomach flops and panic rises in my chest. I stare at her for about three seconds. She is talking on her cell phone; she suddenly turns and looks right at me. I run. I sprint down the street like a mad woman and turn the first corner I see. My hands are shaking and I feel like I am having another hot flash. I gulp several deep breaths of air into my lungs and try to calm myself down. There was no way that Mom had seen me. What the heck was she doing anyway? She was supposed to be in court all day, which in Mom speak usually meant she would be out of sight until at least dinnertime.

I take the long way back to school, behind all of the stores in town where the backstreets are full of garbage and cardboard bins. I cut through the forest on the outskirts of town that connects to the sports fields and track at the high school. I walk along the edge of the soccer field. I impulsively decide that my last classes of the day are not worth going to and sit down on the grass sideline of the field.

My phone buzzes once. I look down to see a text from Emma. "Where R U?"

"Soccer field," My fingers type back on the keyboard.

"Y?"

"Didn't feel like going to class."

"UR funeral." My stomach sinks, reading her last reply, and I know she's right. I didn't make a habit out of cutting school. I knew it wouldn't be long before my mom was calling me and wondering where I was. I push my anxious thoughts aside, lay back on the cold grass and stare up at the cloud-filled winter sky. I might as well enjoy the silence while I can.

FIVE
Kate

I spend the morning in court. A case dealing with fraud. A father and son partnered in a financial planning company together and over the years the son had slowly started taking more than his share. The father had caught him and was suing him. Typically, 80% of the cases I deal with are civil cases. Personal injury, fraud, custody if needed, the list goes on. The rest are criminal cases. Fife Springs is the only town with a courthouse within at least 150 miles each way, so in some instances the cases that come to my docket are from other towns more than my own.

Court recesses for lunch just before noon. I go into my chambers and check my cell phone. I have a message from Duane saying that he'll be a few minutes late. I head to the café we frequent to pick up lunch. Our standing lunch date is at Nora's Café. We'd been going there together since we met. It has amazing coffee, great sandwiches and is quiet and quaint.

I walk through the courthouse doors and my phone rings. "Kate Sherwood." I look right in front of me, not paying any attention to the voice on the other end. Across the street I see my daughter coming out of the pharmacy. Holly looks in my direction and bolts. I can tell by the look on her face that she doesn't think I saw her, so I remain composed. "I'm sorry," I tell the person on the other end of the line. "I'll have to call you back." I hang up the phone and call Gwen.

"Kate," Gwen answers on the second ring. "Aren't you supposed to be in court?"

"Have you heard from Holly today?" I walk down the sidewalk towards the café. The cool January breeze feels refreshing on my skin.

"Why?" Gwen hesitates. I know right away something is up.

"I just saw her walk out of the pharmacy."

"Shit," Gwen sighs.

"Gwen, what's going on?"

"I'm not really allowed to say," she tells me. "Holly came to my office today."

"Is she sick?" I ask. A woman waves at me as I walk past her, and I nod and smile in acknowledgement. "Because I've noticed she's seemed a bit tired lately, off…"

"Kate, I'm not allowed to discuss a patient's medical history with you." Gwen's voice is firm, but I can hear a slight waiver to it.

"She's my daughter, Gwen. She's 16. She's a minor."

Gwen lets out a long sigh. "If I tell you, you can't tell her."

I think about this for a second. "That's fine. I just want to know she's okay."

"Well, she actually came into the office to see Dr. Daniels, but Trudy told me and I went in to see her instead. She came in for a birth control prescription."

As a mother, I'm honestly not sure how I should react in this situation. I instantly feel blindsided. Not about the birth control, I'm glad about that part. At least Holly was being responsible. But what did she need it for? Well, obviously I knew what she needed it for. Did she have a boyfriend? Was she just fooling around with someone? Or was this going to be a random one-time act? Thoughts continue to race through my mind as I reach the café and stop outside the door.

"Katie? Are you okay? Are you still there?" Gwen's voice interrupts my thoughts.

"Sorry," I take a deep breath to stay composed. "Did she tell you what she needs it for? Does she have a boyfriend? I'm confused."

"She told me nothing," Gwen replies. "I talked to her about safe sex and what she needs to do for her sexual health after, but she wouldn't budge on anything else. I'm going to talk to her when I pick her up."

"Okay," I open the door and walk inside. I see Duane, who clearly wasn't going to be as late as he had thought. "Hopefully she gives you something."

"I'll try my best," Gwen says. "Don't worry, Katie. Holly is a smart girl."

"I know," I tell her. "Gwen, I've got to get lunch and head back to court." I sit down at the table across from Duane and he smiles at me.

"Sure," Gwen says. "Tell Duane I say hi." I can't help it. I laugh.

"Will do. Talk tonight." I hang up the phone.

"How's Gwen?" Duane asks.

"She's fine. Sorry, I'm late. I got sidetracked. Did you order?"

"The usual." He nods. "No problem, I wasn't late after all."

I pick up the steaming cup of hot coffee in front of me and take a small sip. I feel slightly disgruntled. I'm typically someone who has all my shit together. Right now I feel like my perfectly composed world has shifted a bit.

"Penny for your thoughts?" Duane whispers. "You seem distracted."

"Gwen told me Holly went to the clinic today to get a prescription for birth control." I tuck a piece of my brown hair behind my ear. "Oh, and I for sure wasn't supposed to repeat that information to anyone."

"Oh," Duane looks mildly uncomfortable at the thought of Holly needing to go on birth control. "I'm guessing she didn't mention it to you? Does she even have a boyfriend?"

"No idea," I sigh. "I'm so tired of battling her. It's getting harder and harder to do alone."

Duane frowns. He doesn't say anything at first. He's just watching me, watching my face. I can tell he wants to reach out to me. To touch me. Put his arms around me. One of our rules is no public contact. Finally he speaks, "I think we should get married."

Those six words are enough to almost destroy me on the spot. My mind starts racing. I instantly feel like any sense of control I had was slipping away. I feel hot. Very hot. I close my eyes.

"Katie?"

I open my eyes. I see Duane staring at me. I feel like I can't breathe. "I need to go," I blurt out. So I do. I bolt out of the café and start jogging. In heels. I run the half a mile all the way to Gwen's office. When I get there everything is spinning and I'm panting. Trudy meets me at the front desk.

"Kate!" She greets me. "Gwen is in her office." I nod, unable to speak, and rush past the desk, past the all of the examination room doors in the sterile, brightly lit hallway. I knock once and open the door.

"Katie," Gwen takes her glasses off of her eyes and looks at me. "What's going –."

"I can't breathe," I spit the words out and don't even know if they are in English. I begin wheezing. Gwen stands up and walks over to me. She grabs me by the shoulders and pulls me forward, sitting me in a chair in front of her desk.

"Katie, look at me." Gwen's voice is soft. "Listen to my voice and look at me." I look into Gwen's eyes. I see Gwen's short blonde curls, defined cheekbones. I see Holly. My chest gets tighter. My stomach churns. "Katie!" Gwen's voice. I close my eyes. "Breathe, babe. Breathe." I listen to Gwen coaching me on my breathing and after a few seconds I begin to slow my breathing to match her pattern. We continue deep breathing for a few minutes and I open my eyes. "Better?" Gwen asks me. She walks over to the mini fridge in the corner of her office, takes out a bottle of water and hands it to me.

"Thanks." I open the water and took a sip. "It's been a long time..."

"What happened?" Gwen asks. She starts to take my blood pressure. I sit very still.

I've had four panic attacks in my life and Gwen has been there for almost all of them. The first was when our parents died. The second was when Holly asked me who her father was for the first time. The third was when Gwen moved to Fife Springs. The forth was today. I'm not usually an anxious person but losing control frustrates me to no end.

I take another sip of water, followed by a deep breath. "Duane told me he thinks we should get married."

Gwen's green eyes go wide, "Seriously?" She uncuffs my arm and places her stethoscope below my shirt on my back.

"Yup."

"Deep breath in." I do as she says. "And out." Gwen moves back around my front and faces me. "And you said?"

"I had to go." Gwen shakes her head. My phone rings. "Ugh. I really have to go. So much for lunch."

"Are you going to be okay?" Gwen asks. " Your blood pressure is a little high."

"I'll be fine," I wave her off. Gwen walks over to me. She wraps me in a tight hug.

"Take it easy, Katie."

"I will," I ease into her hug. I close my eyes, trying not to think of all the secrets wedged deep in the middle of our hug. Secrets that are slowly eating away at me every day. Secrets that I just don't know how much longer I'm going to be able to keep anymore.

SIX
Holly

I'm sitting on the front steps of the school when Gwen pulls up. I jog over to her white BMW, open the door and climb into the passenger seat. I drop my bag on the floor and buckle my seat belt. The doors lock. My heart speeds up a little.

"How was the rest of your day?" She asks, driving out of the parking lot.

"Fine," I stare out the window, not wanting to talk about what I know is coming next.

"What classes did you have?"

I sigh. I don't want to lie. She's going to find out in a few hours anyway. "I didn't go, I hung out on the soccer field." I don't know what I'm expecting to happen, but it's sure as hell not silence. Gwen doesn't say anything for a few minutes.

"I picked up groceries." These are the next words to come out of her mouth. "I was thinking I'd cook tonight. We can do the mall another night?"

"Sure," I say. "I have a lot of homework anyway. What's for dinner?"

"Your grandma's broccoli and cheese soup."

I can't help it, I laugh. Mom and Gwen have always told stories about how growing up grandma would make them her special soup when she wanted to have any type of serious conversation with them. For some reason the soup always got them talking. Grandma's special soup and a sex talk. Sounds like an evening straight out of an after school special.

Gwen drives to my house without another word. The nights that Mom works late, Gwen will usually meet me after school and take me home so I can get started on my homework. She feeds me dinner and we hang out until Mom gets home. This usually happens three to four nights a week.

When Gwen pulls up to the house, I notice a tall boy standing at the gate leading into the courtyard. He is holding a small stack of papers and looks nervous. Short jet-black hair forming the sexiest curls you'd ever seen. I'd recognize that soccer player build anywhere. Why was Griffin Anderson at my house? He wasn't allowed at my house during the daytime hours, that was the rule. I wasn't ready to tell Mom about him and he wasn't supposed to be dating anyone.

"What the heck?" I mutter under my breath as we pull up to the house. Beside me, I see Gwen wearing a small smile on her face. Actually it's more like a smirk.

"Friend of yours?" she asks, innocently.

I don't respond but instead get out of car and walk up to the black aluminum gate that's surrounded by an eight-foot stonewall leading around the house. The wall to both sides of the gate is a pony wall that you can see over into the courtyard that leads up to the front porch.

Our house is beautiful. Mom had it custom built a few years ago. It's a modern build - sleek and sophisticated, just like Mom. The exterior is a cozy stone with massive windows that allow for plenty of natural light throughout the house. The front yard is gorgeous, full of oversized, tranquil trees, and an abundance of flowers. It's her sanctuary. A bit big for the both of us, but Mom had worked hard for it. I still remember the years we'd lived together in a tiny two-bedroom apartment. Mom had been working during the day and taking classes at night. Gwen wasn't in the picture and most of my time was spent with our neighbour Nina and her two kids.

"Hey Holly," Griffin interrupts my thoughts.

"Hi." My eyes could burn a hole through him. I hope he gets the message that I'm unimpressed he's here.

"I brought you your homework." He hands me the papers.

"Thanks." What, were we a couple now? I can feel my face turning fourteen different shades of purple. "I thought you had practice."

"It got cancelled today," Griffin shrugs and runs his fingers through his hair. "Too cold, field is frozen. The season is pretty much over anyway." I hear a car door shut. Gwen who appeared to be giving us some space, walks over to us. If Griffin looked nervous before, he looks like he's going to have a heart attack right now.

"Hi," Gwen says, holding out her hand. "I'm Gwen, Holly's aunt."

He immediately shakes her hand. "Griffin Anderson."

"Right," she responds. "The soccer player. Anderson...I know your mom. Tracy, right?" He nods.

"Well, I should get going," Griffin says, giving me a small smile. "I just wanted to make sure you got your homework. You were on my way home, so it's not a big deal or anything. Nice to meet you, Dr. Sherwood."

"Call me Gwen," she says. "Nice to meet you too." Griffin waves and walks down the front path to the street. He lives a few blocks away.

Gwen puts her hand lightly on my shoulder, "You sure know how to pick 'em, Holly."

I groan. "I don't know what you're talking about."

She ruffles my already ruffled hair. "Come on, let's get you started on that homework."

I spend the next two hours at my desk in my bedroom, engrossed in my homework. First for English, reading and response questions, followed by French vocabulary. The semester is almost over and most of my teachers seem to be piling on the homework and review. Naturally my idea to skip school for the first time ever probably didn't have the most impeccable timing.

By 5:30, I am starving and ready to take a much needed break for dinner – even if it means a Q&A round. I plunk myself down on a barstool at the island. We eat most meals at the kitchen island as it borders the living room. There is a more formal dining room on the other side of the kitchen, but we really only use it when we have company or for special occasions.

Gwen places a plate of salad and a steaming bowl of hot soup in front of me. I pick a red pepper out of the salad and pop it into my mouth. Peppers are my favourite vegetable.

"Thanks," I say. "This looks delicious." I take a bite of the soup. It tastes amazing. I tell Gwen so. We eat dinner in silence. This is very uncharacteristic for the two of us. It's like I'm eating dinner with my mother. Towards the end of the meal I begin to feel slightly anxious and uncomfortable that Gwen still hasn't said anything to me.

When we start to clear the table I can't take it anymore. "Are you mad at me?" I ask her. My heart skips a beat when I do and I notice I start to feel a bit flushed.

Gwen gives me a small smile, "I'm not mad at you, babe. I'm

just not sure what to say. I'm not sure what you'll tell me."

"I'll tell you whatever you want to know," I say the words and I can't believe that I've actually just said them. Honestly though, I'm tired of keeping secrets. I just want to talk to someone. No one knows about Griffin and me, and it would be nice to get some kind of opinion on the subject. "I just don't want you to tell my mom."

"You know that Katie and I don't keep secrets from each other," Gwen tells me for the umpteenth time in my life.

"So basically whatever I tell you...you'll tell her."

"If she asks about it."

"Why would she ask you about my sex life?"

Gwen places her hand over her heart, "I'm going to need some more clarification on those last two words."

"I told you I hadn't –."

"Holly, your mom saw you leaving the pharmacy today." Gwen puts her hand on my arm and gives me a sympathetic look.

"Shit." I sit down on a stool.

"Don't say shit." Gwen sits down beside me.

"So she knows." I feel my chest begin to tighten. I close my eyes.

"She called me and I didn't lie." Gwen shrugs and makes a pained face at me. Panic encompasses my mind and body. I feel myself start to spin. My breathing is picking up and I can't seem to focus anymore. I hear Gwen telling me to breathe. I do what her voice is telling me to and eventually it subsides. "Has this ever happened to you before?" Gwen asks.

"What?" I'm confused. I take a sip of the glass of water she has placed in front of me.

"Sweetie, I think you just had a panic attack."

"Oh, that. Yeah, it's happened a few times in the past few weeks. I can usually get it to stop though."

"Can I tell your mom about that? I might want her to bring you in so we can run a few tests." Gwen tucks a piece of her hair behind her ear. She looks concerned.

"Why?"

"Anxiety runs in our family, it's good to know about it and how it affects you." Gwen stands up, grabs my arm and takes me over to the couch. I think about what she just said. Anxiety runs in our family. Something else no one has ever told me.

"Do you have it?" I ask, sitting down beside her on the

oversized plush couch.

"I used to," Gwen confesses. "When I was around your age into my early twenties."

"Not anymore?"

"I've learned how to control it," she tells me. "It's rare now."

"Does my mom?"

Gwen hesitates, "You should ask her about it." I roll my eyes. These two killed me sometimes. They were like a closed book when it came to one another. Like they had this twin trunk that they kept everything inside of and never let anyone else into.

"Yeah, I'll be sure to do that the next time she's around for a heart to heart." I regret the words the instant I say them. I see a stern look on Gwen's face.

"Holly, that's not –."

"I know," I say. "I'm sorry, I shouldn't have said it. I know she works hard, Aunt Gwen. I know she works hard for me but sometimes I just wish she'd open up to me more. The past few years she's been at a work so much. It's changed her. I wish things were like the way they used to be. I wish that she was more like you."

Gwen sighs, "I'm not perfect, you know. I've got my share of demons." I'd heard her say this before. I had no idea what it meant. I knew that Gwen had gotten into some trouble after their parents had died. I knew she'd had a rough time in college, dropped out for a bit and then eventually gone back, turned herself around and gone to medical school. I knew that her and Mom hadn't talked until I was five years old. I knew I hadn't met her until three years after that. I didn't know why though; no one ever told me why.

"What does that mean?" I ask her.

"Not tonight." She puts a hand on my leg. "Tonight, my girl, is about you. I've let you off for long enough. Tell me about the boy."

I frown. "You mean Griffin?"

Now she rolls her eyes. "Yes, Griffin Anderson, the soccer player. The cute boy who brought you your homework. The cute boy who I'm assuming is the reason you showed up in my office today wanting a prescription for birth control. Why am I assuming this, you ask? Because I've never in all our weekly dates together seen a boy show up at your doorstep. Your mother is one intimidating lady, so I'm guessing this guy really likes you if he's going to risk running into her."

I smile and brush a stray curl out of my eye. "He is cute, isn't he?" She groans and whacks me with a pillow.

"So what's your deal? How long have you been together? Spill it." She manages to look interested and afraid at the same time.

"We've been hanging out for the last month or two. Griffin isn't really allowed to date during soccer season."

"And 'hanging out' means? I'm not down with all the Gen Z lingo."

"I don't know," I shrug. "He usually picks me up late, when Mom's asleep. We go to a park or wherever."

"So this is where the whole sex thing is stemming from. Got it." Gwen purses her lips.

"Yeah," I say. Even though Gwen is cool, I feel uncomfortable. Gwen picks up on this.

"Does it make you uncomfortable to talk about sex?" she asks.

"I guess so. I mean I'd rather talk to you about it than Mom or something, but it's still weird."

"Look Holly, I'm not going to lecture you. You're a smart girl. I just want you to be careful, okay? Having sex before you're ready is never a good idea. I want you to feel like you can always talk to me if you need to. I need you to promise me that you'll be safe. I also need you to know that you can always say no. Never let any guy pressure you into having sex when you're not ready, okay?"

I nod. "Okay. Thanks, Aunt Gwen."

We spend some more time talking. She listens, she offers some advice, and she encourages me to talk to my mom. She hugs me, she loves me but, most importantly, she hears me. I know she's going to talk to Mom about today, but I ignore that for a little while. Right now I just need to be heard. I need hear wisdom. I need to know that I'm making the right decision or that it's okay if I'm making that wrong one.

SEVEN
Kate

I spend the rest of my afternoon in court. All I can think about is getting home, having a long hot shower and washing the stench of the day off of myself. Court adjourns for the day around 5pm. I head into my chambers and take a seat at my large oak desk. I scan my office; the walls are lined with books. On my desk are a laptop, a desk lamp and two pictures. One of Holly and I, and the other of Gwen, Holly and I together.

My phone rings. I see that it is Duane and start to feel my chest tighten. I answer. "Hello?"

"Oh good," Duane sounds relieved. "You answered."

"I just got out of court."

"Can you come over tonight?" He asks. "I want to talk about what happened today."

I swallow hard, feeling a dry lump form in my throat. "I'm supposed to have a meeting tonight. I can cancel it." I don't cancel meetings. Ever. "I'll be there in twenty." I hang up the phone, send out my regrets for the evenings meeting, pack up my briefcase and head out of the office. I say my goodbyes to the few people left in the courthouse entry hall and head outside to my SUV.

It's beginning to get dark already. Duane lives on the opposite side of town from me. I drive to Duane's house and wonder what on earth I am going to say to him. I really don't want to do this. Every part of me wants to turn the car around and drive back home.

My heart aches for Holly. I just want to talk to her. I want to tell her all the things she doesn't know. I don't blame her for not wanting to share things with me; I'm not exactly the greatest role model for honesty.

A few minutes later I pull in to Duane's driveway. Duane lives in a cozy cottage-style rancher. I get out of my car and head towards his front porch. A cool breeze hits me and I shiver in my coat. Duane meets me at the door. He takes me inside, and he wraps his arms around me.

"I'm sorry," he says. I rest my head under his chin, and I melt into his arms. Everything from my day washes away as he holds me.

"I know," I tell him. "I'm sorry too. I just wasn't expecting that."

"I shouldn't have sprung it on you that way," he pulls away and looks into my eyes. His dark brown eyes are so beautiful, so perfect. "I meant what I said though. I want to marry you, Katie."

"I just don't know if I'm ready for that," I admit.

"But you want to marry me?" I think about his question. I want to marry Duane, I do. But it's been just me for so long, I don't even know what that would look like. Then there's Holly – she doesn't even know about Duane and me. Duane takes my hand and leads me into his living room. There are several cartons of Chinese food on the coffee table. "I figured you hadn't eaten."

My stomach grumbles at the sight of food. "I haven't, not since breakfast." He shakes his head and starts making up plates.

"I can't keep doing this," Duane says, sitting down on the couch with his loaded plate of food. "We aren't teenagers, Katie. I want to be in a real relationship with you. I want to take you out, I want to be there for Holly, I want it all." I begin shoveling the food into my mouth to avoid an immediate response. He waits patiently for me to finish.

"I need to tell Holly about us first, Duane," I put my fork down on my plate. "She needs to know before we go any further. Then I'll need to take our public relationship slow for a little while."

Duane grins. "I can agree to that."

"Really?"

"Yes, really." His voice takes on a teasing tone. "I love you, Katie. If you need to move slowly to that next step I'm good with it, as long as we're moving somewhere."

"I love you too." I smile. I feel better. Then I think about telling Holly and it fades. "I hope she doesn't hate me."

"I think she'll be less surprised than you think," Duane offers.

"Oh, is that so?"

"I've been around forever, Katie. Holly is a smart girl. I don't think she'll care if she hasn't already figured it out."

"I hope so," I sigh. Duane puts his plate down on the table, and he pulls me into his arms. He kisses me on the cheek.

"It's going to be okay," he tells me. "I promise." I snuggle into his embrace, praying that he is right.

It's just after seven when I pull into my garage. My plan was to get home before Holly was in bed for once so that we could talk about everything that had happened today. I sit in my car for a few minutes before retreating into the house. I walk through the laundry room, into the foyer and through the kitchen into the living room where Gwen in sitting on the couch reading through a large stack of papers.

"Hey, you're home early," Gwen comments.

"Yeah." I kick off my heels, drop my briefcase on the floor and sit down beside her on the couch. "I cancelled my evening meeting and went to talk to Duane." I fall back into the couch cushions.

Gwen raises her eyebrows. "How uncharacteristic of you."

"I needed to talk to him." I cover my eyes with my hands. "I'm done. Today has been crazy."

"It's not over yet," Gwen's eyes look towards the stairs.

"Is she here?"

"Yeah, she's doing her homework upstairs."

"Did you talk?"

"We did." Gwen fills me in on Griffin, the birth control and the panic attack.

"Griffin Anderson," I shake my head and smile a little. "Girl sure knows how to pick 'em."

"That's what I said!" Gwen laughs.

"Is she feeling okay now?" I frown. Holly had never shown signs of anxiety before. I grab the pillow next to me and hug it against my chest.

"I think so. You should go ask her." Gwen nods towards the stairs. "You need to tell me what happened with Duane first though." I tell her everything that transpired at his house. Her eyes go wide. "WOW! I never thought you'd come around."

I smack her with the pillow. "Thanks a lot!"

"Seriously, Katie. It's been over two years. It's getting ridiculous."

"I'm just worried about what Holly will think."

Gwen laughs. "I'm pretty sure Holly has known about you and Duane forever."

"That's what Duane thinks too." I run my fingers through my hair.

"She was asking about me again tonight." Deep worry lines

appear on Gwen's youthful face.

"What did you say?" I close my eyes again. My head is starting to feel heavy.

"I told her we'd talk about it another day."

"You're going to have to tell her someday." Once the words come out my mouth I want to snatch them back. I'm too tired to fight with Gwen right now.

"We're going to have to," Gwen corrects me. "I wouldn't even know where to begin. She'll hate me." She blinks and I can see that her eyes are filling with tears. She stands up. "Go talk to your daughter." Her words hang in the stale air for a moment too long. I stand up and give her a hug.

"You're amazing, Gwen. I couldn't do any of this without you. I hope you know that." I let go and watch as she wipes the tears off her face.

"Thanks." She begins to gather her papers. "I'm going to head home. We'll talk tomorrow, okay?"

"Yup," I give her a small smile and walk over to the stairs. "Wish me luck." She waves.

I walk up the stairs, past the guest bedroom and stop in the hallway. My room is to my right and Holly's is at the other end of the hallway. I decide to pause our conversation for a few minutes longer. Everything in me needs to get out of these work clothes. In my room I dispose of my clothes and hop into the shower. The hot water feels incredible on my skin. It pounds against my back, washing away all of the tension from the day. I get out of the shower, comb my hair and change into some sweats and a cozy sweater. I slip my feet into my slippers and feel so much better.

It's strange that as a parent some things can still make you so nervous. When I was young, I used to think that by the time I had children of my own I would be this incredible super human immune to emotions like fear and anxiety. If anything, having a child has only escaladed those feelings and made me feel even less in control.

I walk down the hallway and knock on Holly's door. "Come in," she calls. I open the door and walk into her room. Holly is sitting across the room at her desk, which sits in front of a large window.

"Hi there." I walk over to her and give her a kiss on her forehead.

"Hey, you're home early." She gives me the smallest of

smiles. Better than nothing. I sit down on the bed.

"How was your day?" I ask her.

"Crazy!" She sighs, gets up from her chair and throws herself down on the bed beside me. "How was yours?"

"Mine was crazy too. I cancelled my meeting tonight."

"You never cancel a meeting." Holly rolls over to face me.

"I wanted to talk to you." My stomach flip-flops.

"I know. Gwen told me that you saw me today."

I freeze for a second after hearing Holly's words. I felt like an idiot. I was so nervous about Duane that I had almost forgotten what I was supposed to talk to her about. The sex talk. Shit.

"Yeah, but I need to talk to you about something else first." I take a deep breath.

"What?" Holly jumps up looking relieved and concerned at the same time.

"I don't really know how to say this. We've never had it come up before."

"Mom, you're acting weird," Holly points out.

I laugh nervously. "Duane and I...we've been..."

"Seeing each other?" Holly says the words in a matter-of-fact manner.

"You know?" I breathe out.

"Um, I'm pretty sure everyone knows, Mom. You're such a weirdo. You guys should just get married. I don't know why you both act so cloak-and-dagger about everything. I'm not four years old and Duane is a good guy. I like him a lot. Besides, no one in town cares who you date, you guys are both big enough deals that you could squash anyone who bugs you about it like a fly."

I stare at her feeling dumbfounded. I can't help it, I burst out laughing. I laugh and laugh. I fall backwards on the bed and laugh until I can't breathe and tears are streaming down my face. After a few minutes I regain composure and sit back up. Holly is staring at me like I'm possessed.

"Are you okay?" she asks.

"Yes," I let my breath out in a whoosh. "Sorry. I just...all day I have been so stressed about telling you this. I thought you would be so mad at me for keeping this from you. I don't know why I didn't just tell you. It started out that way because I didn't know where it was going and then it just turned into one big long secret...well I guess it wasn't really a secret."

"I want you to be happy, Mom." Holly crosses her legs and sits up straighter. "I really like Duane a lot."

"I guess you aren't a kid anymore," I smile, but it's more of a sad smile than anything.

"Is this where the sex talk begins?" Holly groans.

I shake my head. "You don't need a sex talk. You've been so distant lately; so tired and then with everything that happened today. The birth control, the secret boyfriend, the skipping school." I raise my eyebrows at the skipping of school and watch as Holly bites down on her lower lip. "And Gwen told me you had a panic attack?"

"Apparently it runs in the family," she mutters.

"I had a panic attack today," I admit. I run my fingers through my wet brown hair. Admitting weakness is not my strong suit. Not that anxiety is a weakness; I just don't love the feeling of being overtaken by fear.

"Really? You did?" Holly looks skeptical.

"I did."

"Do you get them a lot?"

"This was the fourth one that I've had in my life."

"Aunt Gwen said she used to get them too, but she wouldn't tell me much."

"Gwen doesn't like to talk about the past."

"Neither do you." Touché.

"So back to Griffin Anderson."

Holly groans. "See what I mean. This is why I didn't want to tell you. I liked that it was a secret. I liked that I had something just for me. Sometimes it feels like you and Aunt Gwen are in this weird twin bubble you both have and then there's just me on the outside looking in. You guys won't share anything about the past with me and you both have all these weird rules and boundaries, but you're like inseparable best friends. I just don't get it."

My mind was racing. Holly wasn't wrong. Gwen and I have always had a very complicated relationship. We were best friends, yes – taking each other's secrets to the grave. But Holly was my daughter and if I had to choose between her and Gwen I would choose Holly in a heartbeat. Gwen knew my past and I knew hers. We understood each other in ways that most people would never get. We had been through the darkest times and come out on top.

"I'm sorry," I finally say, after waiting too long to respond to her. "I can understand how that must be frustrating for you at times."

Holly lies back down on the bed and curls up into a ball. I can tell that this wasn't the answer she was hoping for. "Listen sweetheart." I take her hand in mine, expecting her to pull away, but she doesn't. "I can't give you all the answers you want tonight. I can promise that you'll get them someday though. Right now, I need to be able to trust you and I want you to be able to trust me. Can we start there?"

Holly stares at me for a minute before she speaks. She looks carefully as if she's trying to decide if she believes me or not. "Okay," she finally agrees.

"For you this means no more skipping school. I'd really like to meet Griffin, so if you can promise me that you won't jump into anything yet, I'd appreciate that."

"There's no set timeline, Mom." I can hear the eye roll in her voice. "I just wanted to be prepared, you know, like you taught me." Parenting zing right there.

I don't know what else to say. I want to ask her more about Griffin, but I know that she won't tell me anything. She never tells me much anymore. I'm starting to realize the effect that my job is having on mine and Holly's relationship. It was a lot easier when she was younger and thought the world of me, but now that I had to fight to stay in the good zone it just wasn't working. I make a mental note to see if I can make some changes in my schedule, to try to not work as many late nights and be around more. Now that Holly knows about my relationship with Duane that might make things easier. My job is important, but it's not the most important.

"Well, I guess I'm going to head to bed," I say. I stand up and walk towards the door. I hesitate before saying the next words: "Oh, and you're grounded for skipping school today."

Holly sighs and rolls her eyes at me. "Yeah, I kind of figured I would be."

"Actions have consequences." As soon as I say this I want to kick myself. Holly has never responded well to lecturing.

"Thanks for the tip," she scowls.

I stand at the door for a few seconds, not knowing where to go next. Holly stares at me from her spot on the bed practically challenging me to retaliate. I don't.

"Good night," I say, not looking at her, and leave the room. I walk down the hallway to my bedroom, closing the door behind me. I crawl into my bed, trying to ignore how disconnected I feel with my own daughter. I'm relieved that this long day is finally over.

EIGHT
Holly

I wake up the next morning at 5:30am to my phone dinging. I roll over and see five messages from Griffin. Crap! I throw my head back on my pillow. How had I forgotten about Griffin? After my talk with Mom I'd been so tired I must have fallen asleep.

I type a response back.

HOLLY: Sorry, fell asleep ☹.

My phone dings a few minutes later.

GRIFFIN: I'm outside.

HOLLY: Where?

My fingers quickly tap the touch screen.

GRIFFIN: In your front yard.

I jump up out of my bed; grab a hoodie off my desk chair and sneak down the stairs as quickly and quietly as possible. Before going outside, I go into the laundry room and slip my feet into my slippers. I pull on my hoodie and open the front door. Griffin is sitting on the bench on the porch.

"Are you crazy?" I whisper. "What are you doing here?"

"I was worried about you," he confesses. He stands up and wraps me in a hug. "You didn't respond to any of my messages last night. I know you cut school yesterday and I thought you were mad at me or something." I feel my stomach flip-flop.

"I'm not mad at you." I pull away from him and sit down on the bench. I motion for him to sit down beside me. "I went to the doctor yesterday to get a prescription and my Aunt Gwen found out. Then she told my mom." Griffin looks ill. Add this to the list of reasons I have never had a serious boyfriend. They were usually terrified of my mother.

"So are you in trouble?" Griffin runs his right hand through his hair.

"Not for that. I'm grounded for skipping school though."

"Oh, that's not bad I guess."

"Look, I've been thinking. I don't think I'm ready for sex yet. We aren't even official. I don't want my first time to be like that."

Griffin immediately takes my hand in his. "That's fine, Holly. I'm cool with whatever. I was thinking about talking to my dad about us. Seeing if we could bend his no dating rule."

"Really?" My eyes light up.

"Really." Griffin smiles at me. "I meant what I said, Holly. I love you. I'm crazy about you. I've never cared about that rule until now. No one's ever made me care before." It takes everything in me not to scream like a giddy schoolgirl.

I watch as the front gate opens and Mom walks through it. She's home from her morning run. I suddenly feel nauseous. Griffin sees Mom and looks like about the same as I feel.

"Good morning guys," Mom smiles at us, which surprises me. She still manages to look put together even with her hair in a messy ponytail and skin covered in a thin layer of sweat. "You're up early." She doesn't look angry to see Griffin here, which is even more surprising considering how our talk had gone the night before.

Griffin stands up. "Good morning, your Honour," he stammers. I roll my eyes. I can see that Mom is trying not to laugh.

"Kate is fine. Or Ms. Sherwood if you prefer." She gives him a courteous smile. It's polite and professional.

Griffin nods. "I've got to get to practice." The soccer team did weight training every morning. He looks at me. "See you at school?"

"See you at school."

"Nice to see you, Ms. Sherwood." He runs – no lie – down the pathway and out the gate.

"I'm going to go shower," Mom says, walking past me and into the house. I stand there feeling confused, unsure of what I should do. I decide to let it go. If she's not going to push it, I'll just consider myself lucky. I go inside and upstairs into my bedroom and put of a pair of jeans and a dark green oversized sweater.

Ten minutes later, I'm eating a piece of toast at the island when Gwen walks through the front door. I'm surprised to see her here. "Hey kiddo," she greets me. "What's going on?"

I swallow my last bite of toast. "Not much. What are you doing here?"

"Love you too." She sticks her tongue out at me.

"I didn't mean it like that…I just meant, aren't you supposed to be at work?" I roll my eyes. "So, Griffin came by this morning."

Gwen gives me the tiniest smile. "Oh really?" Her tone is teasing. "What did he want?"

I look behind me to see if Mom is around, but she's still upstairs.

"We were supposed to meet last night..." I look at her to see how she will respond to this. She remains composed. "But I fell asleep right after my talk with Mom and forgot to message him. He was worried and thought I was mad at him."

She still doesn't say anything, just walks over to the coffee maker, pours herself a cup of coffee and lets me talk.

"So I told him what happened yesterday, with Mom and you. And I told him that I wasn't ready, you know, for sex." This grabs her attention; I see one of her eyebrows arch. "And he said that was fine. He told me he loved me again and he said he wanted to talk to his dad about the no dating rule. He wants me to meet his parents."

"He told you he loved you again?" Gwen looks at me.

"That's what you just took from all of that?"

"And that I'm glad you've decided you aren't ready to have sex," she says with a grin. I sigh.

"The other night he told me he loved me for the first time."

"And you told him?"

"Nothing," I groan and throw my body backwards on the bar stool, putting my hands over my face. "What's wrong with me?"

Gwen sits down beside me. "Nothing at all."

"I love you seems like a big deal to me," I tell her.

"It is a big deal," she agrees.

"Do you remember the first time you told someone you loved them?"

She thinks for a moment, "I do. It was my first boyfriend in high school." My ears perk at this reference. Gwen never talks about her past with me. Ever. I wonder about this "high school boyfriend." How long did they date? Why did they break up? As long as I've known Gwen, she hasn't even had a serious boyfriend. I know she's dated but I've never met any of them.

"How did you know?" I ask, wondering if I'm taking this too far.

Gwen takes a sip of her coffee before speaking. "Love is a choice. It's a feeling – yes – but you won't always have that happy, go-lucky butterfly feeling. Real love is deciding to love someone every single day no matter what. It's realizing that they have faults and that you do too but still choosing to love them each and every day regardless." Not exactly the fairy tale answer I was looking for, but still good.

"Sounds complicated."

She smiles. "Maybe sometimes. Sweetie, you're young. You don't need to make that kind of commitment yet – not until you're ready."

"Thanks, Aunt Gwen. You're the best."

"That's what they tell me," she winks.

Mom walks into the kitchen. "Oh good, you're here." She gives Gwen a nod of acknowledgement and heads straight over to the coffee. Adults and their coffee, it's like a lifeline.

"I wanted to ask you both," Mom looks over at us from the other side of the island. "Do you have plans Friday night?" It's Wednesday.

"Don't think so?" My eyes are starting to feel tired already. How do people get up so early all the time?

"I was going to invite Duane over for dinner. I was hoping you could both be there."

"Works for me," Gwen tells her.

"Sure, sounds good," I follow.

"You can bring Griffin if you want," Mom offers.

I scrunch up my lips. "I don't think we're there yet."

"Fair enough." She shakes her head slightly. "Although I think I'd disagree. I've never met anyone who could get you out of bed before seven before."

Gwen laughs.

"Whatever." I roll my eyes at them.

"I've got to get to the clinic," Gwen says. "Holly, if you're ready, I can drive you to school on my way."

"Sure," I tell her. I notice that Mom has a look of concern on her face. I'm not sure what it means or what to make of it. "Is that cool, Mom?"

She nods. "Have a good day. See you tonight."

I wave and run off to grab my bag.

The next few days are somewhat boring. I don't go to any secret doctor appointments or skip any more classes. I manage to avoid any more head-butting sessions with Mom. I basically hang out in the library with Emma, buried in what seems like endless mounds of homework. By the time Friday afternoon rolls around, I'm exhausted. There's a soccer game after school. I know this because Griffin has texted me about it at least six times in the past two days. We hadn't seen each other alone since the morning he showed up outside my house.

"Do you want to come to the soccer game with me?" Emma asks, as she approaches my locker.

"I can probably make it for the first half," I tell her. "Then I need to get home. Duane and Aunt Gwen are coming for dinner."

"Oooo," Emma sings. "The first official 'meet the boyfriend' dinner."

"Except he's Duane and I've known him forever," I say as a matter of fact.

"True." She loops her arm through mine. "Let's go cheer on some Spartans!"

We get to the soccer field a few minutes later and the stands are already filling up quickly. We grab seats in the middle of the crowd of people. The soccer team is already on the field warming up. I see Griffin in the wine-coloured jersey and white soccer shorts. The jersey makes his dark skin look even more flawless. Man, this guy looks good in a uniform. Griffin waves at me. I wave back. Discrete obviously isn't his middle name. Emma is too busy ogling over soccer players to notice.

The first half is uneventful. We are up three to zero by half time. Griffin has scored twice. It's after four, so I tell Emma I have to leave. I send Griffin a text explaining where I've gone and congratulating him on his goals.

I start my twenty-minute walk home. I want to get home before it gets dark. It's also freezing out. I look up at the cloud filled sky and wonder if we will get some snow soon. Fife Springs is usually a sun-and-rain town – it gets chilly in the winter, but never enough for boots and parkas. To get home I have to walk through the heart of the town – we live on the other side. I walk past the courthouse and check for Mom's car, hoping that I can bum a ride if she's still there. No luck. I don't see Gwen's around either. I keep walking, wishing I were wearing more than my medium thick sweater.

I get home and see Gwen's car in the driveway. It's almost dark out. I open the gate and walk up to the door, letting myself inside. The lights are on and I smell something amazing coming from the kitchen. "Hello!" I call, walking towards the kitchen.

"Hi honey," Mom greets me as I approach the island. She's wearing an apron, which reminds me of when I was little and she used to bake for us. Gwen is sitting on a stool at the island cutting up some veggies.

"Hey babe," she says. She puts an arm around my waist and gives me a quick squeeze. "Finally come home to do your part, hey?"

I stick my tongue out at her. "I was at the soccer game."

"Oh really?" Her eyes light up. I roll my eyes in response.

"How was your day?" Mom asks, choosing to ignore Gwen's excitement.

"Meh." I shrug and slide my backpack off, putting it on the floor. "Lots of review packages, lots of studying. Looks like I'm going to have a fun weekend."

"I don't miss that," Gwen comments. She hands me a piece of red pepper and I take a bite of it.

"Yeah." I sit down beside Gwen. "What's with you guys both picking jobs with all this extra schooling? I think I'm just going to skip this whole college thing and go straight into the work force." They both stare at me like I've just told them I'm going to sever my right arm. "Or college sounds good too." I cough and then take another bite of my pepper.

"College is a good place to find yourself, right Gwen?" Mom gives Gwen a knowing look.

"Sure," Gwen says. She looks uncomfortable. Once again I'm confused. Stupid twin bubble.

"When's Duane coming?" I ask.

"Soon," Mom says.

"I'm going to go take a quick shower." They both nod at me and I go upstairs. I shower quickly and change my clothes. I scrunch my hair up with some gel and hear the doorbell ring.

I make it downstairs to see Duane walking into the kitchen. Duane is one of those guys who looks like the lead character in those ridiculous Gourmet Detective movies that Gwen is always making me watch with her. Detective Hollywood. "Holly!" He grins at me and gives me a hug.

"Detective Duane," I joke. I used to call him that when I was a kid. Well, back than he was Officer Duane, but was always protecting me.

"I hear you have a new man friend," he tells me.

I groan. "This conversation is not happening."

"Time to eat!" Gwen interrupts us. So we do. Dinner is incredible. Mom cooked up a roast with all the trimmings. It's funny how you can forget how good someone's cooking is. Mom doesn't cook much anymore, but when she does, she could give Martha Stewart a run for her money.

Dinner is also a lot of fun. It's natural to see Mom and Duane together. Mom seems relaxed and happy, and I'm happy for her. I help clean up after dinner and dessert, and then claim I need to start my homework. I get a text from Griffin telling me he's outside. What was with this guy? I slip out the front door hoping that I'm unseen.

"Griff! You really need to stop –" I'm interrupted when his lips meet mine. The kiss is passionate. His lips are cold against my warm ones and it makes my skin tingle. I pull away.

"I've wanted to do that for the past three days," he confesses. "I can't stop thinking about you, Holly." He grabs my hips and swings me around to sit on the bench. He sits beside me and starts kissing me again. Honestly, I have limited self-control when it comes to kissing Griffin Anderson. I get lost in his kisses. We kiss for a while before I break away.

"Griff," I say. "We shouldn't do this here." He kisses me neck. My cheek. And he's back to my lips. I sigh and melt into the kiss. I'm so wrapped up in emotion that I don't even hear the front door open. I hear Duane clear his throat, and I spring up from the bench. Duane, Mom and Gwen are standing there staring at us. Duane looks like he's going to burst out laughing, and Mom and Gwen both look slightly horrified.

"And that's my queue," Duane gives Mom a quick kiss and winks at us. "Have a good night kids!" He walks down the walkway.

"I should go," Griffin stammers and follows Duane. I stand there rocking on my heels, unsure of what to say or do.

"That's some homework assignment," Gwen says, breaking the ice.

"Inside!" Mom grabs my hand and pulls me towards her into the house.

"Sorry?" I offer meekly.

"For?"

"Kissing Griffin?"

"Oh babe, you never need to apologize for kissing a boy," Gwen says.

Mom rolls her eyes. "Gwen, maybe you should go."

Gwen shrugs. If she looks hurt she doesn't show it.

"Fair enough." She gives me a quick hug. "Good luck, kiddo. See you tomorrow."

"I'm sorry," I blurt out again, as soon as Gwen is gone. "Griffin texted me saying he was outside again and then he started kissing me and…"

Mom holds up her hand to stop me. "First, you don't need to keep apologizing. I get that you're a teenager and you have hormones." I gag when she says the word hormones. "BUT – second, we are going to need to have some house rules about boys."

"What do you mean house rules?" I follow her over to the couch and sit down beside her.

"I just feel like we need some ground rules," Mom sighs. "We've never had boys – 'men' – over much before. I'm fine if you and Griffin want to hang out here. Just not without Gwen or I home and the door needs to be open."

"Okay," I say this probably not in the most open way.

Mom gives me a look that tells me to stop copping an attitude. "I'm not going to spy on you, Holl. I'll give you your privacy. I would just appreciate it if you respected these rules. I get that you guys want to explore and all of that –." I think the horrified look on my face when she uses the word "explore" tells her otherwise. "But sex has consequences. You of all people should know that."

"Right. Consequences…" I feel a slight pang in my chest. I know that most women probably don't dream of being a single parent. We've never talked about it before, and it drives me crazy.

"You know what I mean," she says gently. "Don't take what I'm saying the wrong way. Being a single mom, it was one of the hardest things I've ever done. With that being said, you are also the greatest joy of my life. I just want you to be smart, and I want you to be careful. Can you do that?"

"Fine." I give her a fake smile. "So does that mean no boys over for you when I'm not home?"

She shakes her head at me. "Smart ass."

"That's me." I give her a real smile this time. "Okay, can I actually go do my homework now?" She nods and off I go.

NINE

Kate

The next two weeks go better than expected. I'm able to get into a groove at the office and at home. Finally. I'm not sure where I'd gone the past few years. Holly was a good kid, she didn't need me constantly holding her hand and, thankfully, Gwen had always been more than helpful when I needed her. I'd always felt the pressure of being a career woman and a single parent (or even just a mother), but I'd never realized that when I finally made it to where I wanted to be that I was the one who got to call the shots.

Realizing I was in control, I made an effort to start prioritizing better and relinquishing some small amounts of responsibility to others in my circle. These were hard things for me to do, but doing them meant that I got to spend more time at home with Holly. It meant I got to go out on regular dates with Duane – which, by the way Holly was right about: no one even batted an eye at us.

I get a text from Holly, asking if I'm at work. It's 3:30 and I'm just about to head home. I have some paperwork to do, but I plan on finishing it at night when Holly will be doing her homework. She was really feeling the pressure with the semester ending and exams beginning the following week. I'm about to text back, but decide to call her from the car instead. I collect my things, walk out into the courthouse lobby and see Holly sitting on a bench waiting for me. She has her hands clasped together and is tapping her right foot on the floor. She looks nervous.

"Hey," I say as I approach her.

"Hi. Aunt Gwen had an appointment. She told me to see if you could drive me home."

I nod. "Sorry, I just read your message. I was going to call you from the car."

"Griffin's dad wants me to come over for dinner tonight," Holly spits the words out. Her eyes are wide and she looks stressed. "What am I supposed to do?"

I laugh and sit down on the bench beside her. "Go," I say

gently. "It will be good." I'm surprised that she's come here to talk to me about this instead of Gwen.

"I'm scared," she admits. In that moment, I realize how young Holly is – how limited her experiences are.

"It's okay to be scared." I rest my hand on her arm. "Fear is a natural and normal reaction. Just as long as you don't let that fear stop you from doing what you're supposed to do."

"I just don't know what to say," Holly tells me. "Griffin told me that his dad said we could date. He just wants to meet me officially."

"What about his rules?" I'm curious. Gwen had filled me in on the dating rules of the Anderson family during soccer season.

"Apparently they were just so Griffin wouldn't play the field like every other jock at our school. Once he found out it was me he was totally fine with it." Holly grins. "I guess I should thank you for that. Being the judge's daughter has its perks." She isn't wrong.

"It can also have its disadvantages," I point out.

"Don't I know it." She composes herself back to serious Holly. "Really though, Mom. I don't know what to do. I don't know what to say. I feel like I'm going to throw up."

"Let's go home," I suggest. "We can come up with a game plan on the way. What time are you supposed to be there?"

"Six."

"Plenty of time. You'll be just fine!"

"Do you remember the first time you met your boyfriend's parents?" Holly asks, once we are in the car.

I think about this for a moment. I don't remember. I'd only ever had three serious boyfriends. "My high school boyfriend and I had known each other since we were kids. I dated a guy in college but nothing too serious, and then Duane." I had actually met Duane's parents before but we hadn't been dating so it wasn't a big deal. His mom had called me last week squealing with delight that we had finally "figured things out," as she put it.

"What about my dad?" Holly asks. I freeze. "Didn't you two date?"

"Not his parents either," I say quickly. I look straight ahead. I wonder if she's caught me. I can't believe I slipped up like that. I've always known it would happen one day. The shadow of that coming day has haunted me for the past sixteen years.

Holly doesn't say anything. This makes me extremely

nervous. I look down at my hands, separating my fingers and slowly joining my finger tips together, starting from my pinkies to my thumbs. This was an exercise I'd learned a long time ago to help me reset myself when feeling anxious.

"You just need to be yourself," I tell her. "You already know you've made a good impression if his dad is willing to bend his rules for you."

"True," she says, staring out the window. I know she's thinking about her dad. I know she's wondering. I know she wants to ask. I know she's scared of what I will or won't say. I hurt for her. I wish I could just explain everything to her. I'm so tired of doing this.

"I'm sorry," I whisper in the smallest voice. I say it so quietly that I don't even know if she hears me.

She doesn't say anything and looks away. I feel like this is continuously happening in my relationship with Holly. We break down a few walls and she starts to open up, but then something from my past gets in the way and brings us right back to square one. I can only think of one way to fix this and I'm ready to make it happen.

We get home and I can see Holly finally starting to relax. She doesn't give me the cold shoulder but I can tell she's not happy with me. I help her pick an outfit and get ready, then I drive her to the Andersons' house.

"Griff can probably walk me home after," she says.

I nod. "Good luck. Call me if you need me." I move towards her to hug her, but she pulls away and gets out of my car. I sigh and feel an immediate jab of rejection. I watch her walk to the door and feel a little nervous for her myself. Holly is great with people and I know she will make a wonderful impression on Griffin's parents. I wait until she's inside and drive to Gwen's place.

Gwen lives in a swanky condo building about seven minutes from my house but just outside the town line. She lives in a penthouse suite on the tenth floor. The building is mostly full of working professionals, so it's quiet but a very trendy place to live. I buzz myself in and take the elevator up to her floor.

I knock and she opens it almost instantly. Her blonde curls are up in a messy topknot, she is wearing reading glasses, sweats and an oversized plaid shirt. "I didn't know you were coming over," she says.

I shrug. "Neither did I."

She motions for me to come inside. Gwen's apartment is beautiful. White walls and cabinets with splashes of colour everywhere. Gorgeous marble counter tops and white oak flooring. Nothing ever looked out of place. I take a seat on her navy blue couch and notice a stack of papers spread out along the coffee table.

"I'm just doing some research," she explains. "Do you want some wine?" I nod. Gwen, like me, isn't much of a drinker. She will have an occasional drink a few times a year, but her stock is never ending. Gwen told me it's common for patients to give their doctors alcohol – especially at Christmas time. Maybe they think they need the buzz or something.

She walks over to the adjoining kitchen and takes a bottle of red wine off the rack. She opens it with a bottle opener and pours us both a glass.

"Thanks," I say, when she hands me the glass and sits down beside me.

"Something tells me this isn't a social call," Gwen says. I realize I haven't seen Gwen in a few days. This is uncommon; Gwen has to drive past our house to get to her office so she usually stops by at least once a day, sometimes twice. She looks off to me. Her eyes have dark circles under them. She looks exhausted – like she hasn't slept in days.

"Are you okay?" I touch her arm lightly. "You look really tired."

"Yeah," Gwen yawns in response. "I am. I've been working a lot, studying, doing research. I'm working on this paper that I'm trying to get published." She still seems funny to me, but I let it go. That's not why I'm here.

"Holly asked me about her dad today."

Gwen takes a sip of wine and clamps her lips shut. I hate it when she turns into Bitch Gwen. It's a side of her that only seems to come out around me.

"Don't be like this," I can feel myself starting to get frustrated.

Gwen gives me a hard stare. "What did you say?"

"I said nothing, Gwen!" I put my glass down on the coffee table. "What am I supposed to say? This is ludicrous."

"You promised."

"I don't care anymore. She's sixteen." I feel myself becoming agitated.

"She's going to hate me."

"She won't."

"She's going to hate you." Gwen's eyes could burn a hole through me.

"She won't." My tone is firm. "I need you to figure this out, Gwen. It was never supposed to be this way. We aren't doing this forever. I can't keep lying. She almost caught me in one today."

"Be more careful then." Gwen's voice sounds almost venomous. This is very uncharacteristic of her. I am suddenly filled with such a rage; I know that I need to leave. I get up. "What are you doing?" she asks.

"I can't be here," I tell her.

"Don't be dramatic."

"I put my whole life on hold for you Gwen!" I shout the words at her. "I gave up everything for you. So don't sit here and tell me to be more careful. How about you grow a pair and start being honest with everyone?" I rarely shout. I rarely lose my temper either. I hate the feeling of being out of control.

"Sorry your life is such a burden," Gwen snorts. "You're so hard done by – a judicial position, a beautiful daughter, a mansion."

"That's not what I mean and you know it." I take a deep breath. "I'm still in the dark, Gwen. There are things I should know and I don't."

"You were right," she says. She walks over to the door and opens it. "You should go."

"Fine." I walk over to the now open door and walk out without saying another word. I drive home feeling exhausted and defeated. I love Gwen, she was my only sister, and my twin, and we had been through a lot together. But I'd spent far too long living on the brink of her bad choices. In this moment all I wanted to do was talk to my mom. Sometimes that wave of loneliness hit me hard.

We were only eighteen when our parents died. It hit both of us in different ways. I took comfort in our home, my friends and my boyfriend. Gwen had gone away to college, while I had deferred my first year. I stuck around town, boxed up and sold my parents things and sold their house – which had been enough to pay for the majority of both of our educations.

Gwen had gone down another path. At college she'd discovered the world of partying and drugs. She'd gone on a bender for months. There had been times where she had come home so strung out that I almost didn't recognize her. It was a miracle she managed not to drop out of school. I started college while Gwen continued on her path. Then Holly came into the picture. I was half way through my bachelor's degree and started taking night classes. I had some amazing friends and neighbours who gave me practically free childcare. Gwen and I didn't speak for five years.

I'll never forget the day she showed up in Fife Springs. I'd finished law school two years before and had gotten a job at the only law firm in town. The pay was almost nothing but I'd heard good things about Fife Springs, and I'd wanted to get Holly into a good school with good roots. It was important to me that we lived somewhere family oriented and that was our town. The crime was low, the schools were good and the people were welcoming – it met my "mom checklist."

When Gwen first showed up in Fife Springs, I had just about lost my mind. I hadn't seen her in so long. We'd just briefly started connecting again for obligatory holidays. E-mail at Thanksgiving, a phone call at Christmas and our birthday.

Was she okay? What did she want? Was she clean? Those were the questions that ran through my mind when Gwen showed up on my doorstep many moons ago. Gwen had just finished medical school. She had been accepted to do her residency at the hospital in town. This wasn't a coincidence; she had been keeping tabs on me and wanted to reconnect. I was terrified.

Holly was smitten with Gwen. Gwen had always been the fun, easygoing one. She took a drug test and I let her stay with us for a few weeks. I told her she had to find her own place if she was going to live in our town. She couldn't live with us. Some people may have thought I was a dragon lady for this, but I had my reasons. It had taken us years to get to the place we were at now. Gwen had broken my trust, and trust wasn't something you could just get back in an instant.

I pull into my driveway feeling shaken and frustrated. I go in through the garage and into the kitchen. I should probably eat something but my conversation with Gwen has reduced my appetite to nothing. I pour myself a glass of water and go upstairs to my bedroom. I change into my pajamas, get into bed and turn on the TV. I don't watch a lot of television; I think it's a waste of time. There were many years where we didn't even have a TV because I couldn't afford cable.

I find some lovey dovey made-for-TV movie and, two hours later, I am lying in bed sobbing at the end of it. All I can think about is Holly. I don't want her to hate me. I wonder what will happen if she ever finds out the truth – the unforgiveable sin that binds Gwen and I together. I finally pull myself together when Holly texts me saying that she is on her way home.

"Mom?" I hear her call from the hallway.

"In here!" I call from my room, still in bed.

She walks in the door and takes a look at me. "What's wrong? Are you okay?"

"I'm okay," I say. "Just tired."

"You look upset."

I don't think Holly has ever seen me cry before. I'm not big on crying – I also view it as a waste of time. I wipe the tears from my eyes. "Sorry sweetie, this movie just got the best of me." I motion towards the TV screen.

"Right." Holly looks concerned.

"I'm serious. It's just been a long day. I need to get some rest. How was dinner?" I attempt to change the subject and hope that she takes the bait.

"So good!" she squeals. She goes on to recreate the entire dinner for me. His parents loved her. They had also set some ground rules for the two of them – mostly in regards to how much time they were spending together. They wanted to get together for brunch soon. Griffin had officially asked her out on the way home. I'm happy for my girl and so proud of her. I tell her so. Holly heads off to bed and I immediately fall into a deep sleep.

Gwen and I barely speak to each other for the next few days. Besides our brief exchanges when she's with Holly or text messages about Holly, that's it. We don't talk, and we barely acknowledge one another. Holly doesn't mention it to me and I'm not sure if Gwen has mentioned anything to her.

It's Tuesday morning and I'm in the middle of an arraignment when the bailiff approaches me at the bench. He hands me a piece of paper. *"Gwen's been taken to the hospital. Urgent."* My stomach sinks. I bang my gavel down. "Sorry, counsellors. I have a family emergency. Court's adjourned." I stand up and head for my chambers. I remove my robes, grab my purse and run.

TEN
Holly

I'm in the middle of my French final. It's my last final of the semester. The classroom phone rings and I'm in such a grove of adverbs and tenses that I barely notice. Madame Crowe comes over to my desk. "Holly," she says. "You need to go to the office."

I'm confused. I'm writing an exam. "But what about –."

"You can finish your exam later," she gives me a sympathetic smile.

I hand her my examination booklet, grab my bag and leave the room. My locker is empty so I don't stop there first. I get to the main office and see Mom standing at the doors waiting for me.

"Aunt Gwen's in the hospital," she says. "I've signed you out for the day."

"What do you mean?" I ask her. She is already heading out the front doors and I jog after her to keep up.

"I really don't know much," her voice is strained. I note how stressed she looks. My mom is a very composed person in public; she doesn't show much emotion and she always looks professional. She's told me many times that a big part of her job is how she's perceived on a day-to-day basis. We get to her car and she starts driving before I even have a chance to get my seatbelt on. "I was in court and got a note that Gwen was in the hospital. I called her office on my way here. Trudy told me that Gwen collapsed at work. That's all I know."

I have a bad feeling. These past few weeks, Gwen has seemed different. Tired, distracted, not like her normal self at all. She'd told me that her and Mom had gotten into a fight. I didn't know what it was about, I noticed how off it had made her, but I was too nervous to say anything to Mom about it. I knew Gwen had struggled with addiction in her past, and I had never seen her like this before.

The twenty-minute drive to the hospital seems to take a lifetime. Mom looks frantic as she tries to find a parking spot and pay. We head in through the main entrance together. The hospital is small but recently renovated. Mom walks right up to the front desk. "I'm looking for my sister, Gwen Sherwood," she says to the lady at the desk. "She should be in emergency."

The woman types something on the keyboard into her computer. "Yes. Gwen Sherwood, Pod 8. Just go through the doors on your right and turn left at the end of the hall." She points to the doors that she's talking about.

Mom nods and starts walking. I follow her. When we get to the pod I look through the glass doors and see Gwen lying on a bed inside. Her eyes are closed. She's unconscious? Sedated?

A nurse walks by. Mom introduces herself and explains who she is. A doctor appears in less than two minutes. Mom has that kind of effect on people. Mom and the doctor go into Gwen's room. Mom tells me to wait outside. I feel like I'm in some weird alternate reality. I text Griffin and tell him what's going on. Then I text Emma. They are both in exams, so I don't expect a response. I sit on a chair in the hall, and I wait. They've closed the curtain so I can't see inside.

After ten minutes, the doctor comes out. Mom is still in the room. I wait some more. Five minutes later, Mom comes outside. "You can come in. She's awake. And she's okay." Her tone is reassuring. I follow Mom into the pod. I see Gwen lying in the bed, looking as pale as ever. She has dark circles under her eyes. Her lips are dry and her usually bouncy hair looks as flat as a pin.

"Hey babe," she croaks out the words. "Sorry I freaked you out."

"How are you feeling?" I ask.

"I'm okay," she says. "I'm just waiting on a few more test results and then we'll know more." I grab her hand and squeeze it. I've never been in a hospital room before. I've never had a reason to be. It smells awful and looks dirty and clean at the same time. Sterile, but gross.

"Are you guys friends again?" I ask the sisters. Mom gives me an amused look.

"We'll be okay," Gwen says quietly.

A doctor comes back into the room. "Your test results are back, Gwen." He looks at Mom and I. "Maybe we should do this alone."

"Sweetie, can you go grab me and your mom some coffee?"

Gwen gives me a reassuring smile. I look at Mom.

"It's okay, Holly. I'll tell you when we're done." Mom takes her wallet out of her purse and hands me a crisp twenty-dollar bill. She touches my shoulder as I walk past her and out of the room.

I wander the beige-gray hospital looking for somewhere to get food. I find a small coffee shop near another entrance. I order myself a coffee and a cinnamon bun. I sit down and take a bite of the most delicious cinnamon bun that I've ever tasted in my life. It's the perfect amount of gooey with just the right balance of icing and no raisins as far as I can see. When I get nervous, I stress eat. I sit there for a while, wondering what could be wrong with Gwen. The fact that they wanted me to leave meant nothing – Gwen could have a broken ankle and they would probably want to talk about it without me first. That's just the way that they were – twinish. I sit there for a while longer, finish my coffee, order two more and head back to the ER wing.

ELEVEN
Kate

"Gwen, your tests show that you have a form of cancer called leukemia."

Cancer. I hear the word and my heart sinks in my chest. I stand beside Gwen who closes her eyes and takes a deep breath. I take her hand in mine.

"I don't have cancer," my sister says. "That's ridiculous. I'm just tired. Over worked."

"We're running a few more tests to figure out the type of leukemia and then we can set you up with an oncologist to get you started on a course of treatment. I'm so sorry."

"Let me see," Gwen says to the doctor, who looks uncomfortable with this request. "Show me my labs."

"Gwen," I cut in. "He's just trying to do his job…"

"Let me see the damn labs," she says. "And I want to talk to Dr. Anderson." Gwen turns to me. "Dr. Anderson is the head of oncology."

This doctor now looks extremely uncomfortable. He hands Gwen his tablet with her charts. She begins examining the screen. "I'll go see if I can find Dr. Anderson," he says, stumbling over his words, and then leaves the room.

"Gwen," I say. She doesn't respond. "Gwen! What are you doing?"

"These young doctors don't know what they're talking about."

"Gwennie, you're a young doctor."

"You're not helping." She was right.

"Holly will be back soon," I place my hand lightly on Gwen's arm. "She's going to want to know something. What are we going to tell her?"

"We can tell her I'm overtired. That my iron was low." Gwen's jaw is hard and her mouth has taken the shape of an uncharacteristic scowl.

"We can't lie to her, Gwen," I sigh a heavy sigh. "We've

already lied to her enough."

A woman in her late 40s walks into the room. She's wearing scrubs but still manages to look completely flawless. Her skin is a deep caramel bronze, the colour of light coffee beans. Her black hair is pulled up into a tight, smooth ponytail. She greets us both with a smile.

"Dr. Gwen Sherwood." She walks over to the bed and takes both of Gwen's hands in hers. "Dr. Porter has gotten me up to speed with your file." She turns to me, "Hi, Kate." I blink my eyes and realize that it's Tracy Anderson standing in front of me. Tracy is Griffin's mom. We've crossed paths a few times at different school functions over the years.

"Tracy!" I hold out my hand to her. "Sorry, it's been a long day. I'm not used to seeing you in scrubs."

"Understandable," she gives me another small smile. "Is Holly here?"

"She's just getting coffee," Gwen says. "She doesn't know anything yet. Just that I fainted."

"You looked over your blood work?" Dr. Anderson asks Gwen. Her face shows sympathy. Gwen nods in response. "Your blood work and scans show that you have leukemia. We will have to run a few more tests to determine the subtype. I'd suggest a bone marrow biopsy as soon as possible. Once we know more, we can determine the best treatment plan for you. I'd like to keep you here for a couple of days while we finish running those tests. You'll need to be readmitted later for the first few days of your chemotherapy if that's the course of treatment we decide to take."

"Is the success rate high?" I ask, feeling like a moron with two doctors in front of me.

"It depends on the type of leukemia," Gwen says before Dr. Anderson can speak.

"Yes," Dr. Anderson confirms. "Once we narrow that down, we will have a much better look at things." She puts her hand on Gwen's shoulder. "Let's get started so we can crush this, okay?"

"Deal," Gwen whispers.

"I'll be back in a little bit," Dr. Anderson excuses herself and leaves the room.

"I'm so sorry, Gwen." I say. I feel a slightly stupid for apologizing, but I don't know what else to say to her. This is all moving very fast.

Gwen closes her eyes. "I guess that's just how life works. Go to medical school to save lives. Get cancer and lose your own instead." She sounds bitter.

"You're not going to die, Gwen." I'm terrified. I don't know what I would do without Gwen. There's a knock at the door. Holly sticks her head inside the room.

"Can I come in?" she asks. I notice that she looks pale and stressed.

"You can come in." My eyes are on Gwen who sinks back into her raised pillows even more.

"What did the doctor say?" Holly asks. She sounds like she is trying to walk on eggshells.

"Nothing much," Gwen replies quickly. "I've just been really overworked –."

"I saw Dr. Anderson," Holly interrupts her. Part of me wants to high-five her for being so blunt. The other feels a pang of sympathy for Gwen. "They don't usually send an oncologist to see an overworked person."

"Holly," I start to say, but she quickly cuts me off.

"Just forget it." She looks hurt and alone on the other side of the room.

It feels like hours before Gwen finally speaks. "Come here, Holly," she says, motioning my daughter towards her hospital bed.

Holly walks over to Gwen. She sits on the edge of her bed. I watch as Gwen takes Holly's hands in hers. My heart starts racing a little bit. I wonder what she's going to say.

"I have cancer," Gwen says. She looks into Holly's eyes. Gwen's eyes are filled with tears. Holly's entire face crumbles. "Dr. Anderson was here to confirm the test results. I have leukemia. They need to run some more tests to figure out the subtype. I'll be here for a few more days and then they will figure out the best treatment for me."

I look at Holly and wonder what she is thinking. No one close to her has even been sick before. I don't think she's even ever been in a hospital before. She doesn't cry, she just stares down at Gwen's hands.

"Do you have any questions?" Gwen asks her softly. I watch her reach out and tuck one of Holly's loose blonde curls behind her ear. I have to hand it to Gwen – she is extremely calm and composed. Granted, part of this is second nature to her; delivering bad news is part of her job. Gwen has always been like this. She's calm and understanding and almost always knows the right thing to say in any situation.

"When will the treatment start?" Holly asks in a small voice, almost a whisper.

"Likely next week," Gwen tells her. "Leukemia can be aggressive, so treatment tends to move quickly."

"Holl," I say, "I think I should get you home. You can come back and see Gwen tomorrow. We'll probably know more then."

"That's a good idea," Gwen agrees. She takes Holly in her arms and pulls her close. She whispers something in her ear that I can't hear. For a second, I'm jealous of their closeness. The moment between the two of them is so intimate that I feel like I should leave. When she finally pulls away, I give Gwen a hug and tell her I can come back later if she'd like. Holly and I leave the room together.

We walk through the hospital and she is silent. I watch her out of the corner of my eye, wondering what to say, how she's feeling, if she's okay, what she's thinking. We get outside and the cold air hits my cheeks. I shiver. I turn and realize Holly is no longer beside me.

I look back and see her standing in front of the automatic glass doors. Tears are streaming down her cheeks. She is shaking. I get an awful pit-like feeling in my stomach and walk back towards her. I move her away from the doors and wrap my arms around her. She rarely lets me touch her anymore and the happiness that I feel from this moment makes me feel guilty that it's on Gwen's behalf. She immediately starts crying ever harder. Loud, ugly sobs emerge from my little girl and my heart breaks for all the pain that she is feeling right now.

"Shhh," I whisper into her hair, kissing the top of her head.

"I don't want her to die," she sobs out the words with loud, short breaths in between them.

"I know," I tell her. "It's going to be okay." I say those words wishing I could believe in their absoluteness but I'm not so sure. I don't know that it's going to be okay. Not one little bit.

It's well past dinnertime by the time we get home. I offer to make some food for Holly but she says she's not hungry and retreats to her room.

I'm rummaging through the kitchen trying to find something

edible to eat when the doorbell rings. I walk from the kitchen through the foyer and open the door. Duane is standing there in a fitted grey v-neck sweater, black leather jacket and jeans, looking as good as ever. My eyes wander to the bag in his hand. "I figured you could use some dinner." He gives me a sympathetic smile. I had called Duane earlier and let him know what was going on with Gwen.

I throw my arms around him and plant a kiss on his lips. "Have I ever told you how much I love you?"

"Not today," he admits.

"Well you're the best," I tell him. We head inside to the kitchen and he starts to unpack the food.

"Will Holly want any?" He asks.

I shake my head. "I don't think so. She said she wanted to be alone."

"Poor kid," he says, spooning some of the Pad Thai onto my plate. He had no idea.

We eat at the island together. Duane tells me his parents are coming to visit next month and want to get together with Holly and I. I tell him more about Gwen and what Dr. Anderson said. When we finish eating and decide we are going to watch a movie, Holly comes downstairs.

"Hi sweetheart," I call out to her. "Duane brought over some Thai food if you're hungry."

"Sure, that would be great," she says. "Thanks, Duane." She gives him a quick hug and sits down at the island. I hand her a plate.

"How are you feeling, kiddo?" Duane asks her.

"I'm okay," she shrugs. "I just slept for a bit. Mom, Madame Crowe emailed me and said that she's omitting the last part of my French exam. It was oral. I guess I only got one question wrong on the rest of the test, so she's going to average my mark based on that."

"That's nice of her," I say. "So you're done then?"

"Yes," Holly says. "No school for the rest of the week." I wonder if that was a good thing or not. Sometimes distraction could be a lifesaver.

"We were just going to watch a movie," Duane tells her. "You want to watch?"

Holly sucks in the inside of her cheek and thinks for a few seconds. "Sure."

I'm surprised by her answer. Duane picks a movie. Some action shoot-'em-up film. The three of us sit on the couch, Duane with his arm around me and Holly hugging a pillow so tightly that I think it will burst open. It feels so perfect, the dynamic of the three of us. It's so natural and normal. I wonder why I spent so many years afraid of this, a relationship that all along had been so right.

Gwen calls me early the next morning and tells me that she is going in for her bone marrow biopsy. They should have the results back within a day. Those 24 hours feel like the longest 24 hours of my life. I go back and forth from the courthouse, to home, to the hospital. Holly is at the hospital for most of the day. She doesn't say much; she just wants to be as close to Gwen as she can. We are back home when Gwen finally calls to tell me her test results are in; Holly begs to come with me. I know Gwen won't want her there. Gwen will want to shelter the news as much as she can but I can't seem to give Holly a good reason otherwise, so she comes.

When Holly and I walk into Gwen's hospital room together, Gwen gives Holly a sideways glance.

"Hey Holl," Gwen embraces her in a quick hug. "I didn't think I'd see you back here today."

"I wanted to be here."

"I'm glad you came," Gwen squeezes her hand. I know she's lying. She's pissed that I brought her. Gwen is very similar to me in the sense that she likes control. She likes to be the dealer of the cards.

Dr. Anderson comes into the room. "Hi Kate," she smiles at me. "Holly! Good to see you. Is everyone staying for this?" She cocks her head in Holly's direction.

"Sure," Gwen says in a funny, high-pitched voice.

"Okay," Dr. Anderson sits down on Gwen's bed. "Your test results show that you have acute myeloid leukemia." My eyes are on Gwen. I watch her face and try to read her blank expression.

"Well, that's not the worst news you could have given me," Gwen replies.

Dr. Anderson nods and puts her hand on top of Gwen's for a brief moment. They have a silent exchange between the two of them that goes under my twin radar. Then she turns to Holly and me. "Normally, white blood cells help fight infection and protect the body against disease. When a person has leukemia, it's a bit different. Their white blood cells turn cancerous and multiply when they shouldn't, resulting in too many abnormal white blood cells, which then interfere with the body's ability to work as it should. In acute myeloid leukemia, too many immature white blood cells – called myeloid blasts – are made. What that means is that these leukemia cells are abnormal and cannot mature into normal white blood cells."

"So how do you fix it?" Holly asks. "I mean, can you fix it?"

"Chemotherapy," Gwen answers.

"Yes," Dr. Anderson confirms. "So Gwen will have to stay here for a few days. We will give her a shorter round of chemotherapy that will lower her blood cell count right away. Then she can go home with you for a few weeks. Gwen, you'll need to be with people who can take care of you." She says this firmly, like it's not up for discussion. "Then you'll need to come back for another round of induction chemotherapy. You'll likely be here for one to two weeks. We will see how your body responds to treatment and if any obstacles occur."

"The best case scenario is that I will go into remission after that and then will still need to continue outpatient treatment to prevent a relapse," Gwen tells Holly gently.

"You've done your homework," Dr. Anderson nods, impressed.

"I like to know what's going on inside my body," Gwen replies.

"Don't we all," I say. I look at Holly. I can tell that she's processing. I wonder if Gwen is being more optimistic because she's here, or if she's giving us the whole truth.

"Holly," Dr. Anderson interrupts my thoughts. "Do you have any questions for me?"

"Is the chemo going to make you really sick?" Holly says almost in a whisper, looking at Gwen. "Are you going to lose your hair?"

"Come here," Gwen pulls Holly towards her. "It might. Chemo can have some brutal side effects, but I don't want you to worry about that now. We can cross that bridge when we come to it." She pulls her into a tight hug. "It's all going to be okay. I'm just going to need you to come keep me company while I'm stuck here. Can you do that?" Holly nods in response. "Good."

I watch their embrace and close my eyes, trying not to

imagine what the next few weeks will bring.

TWELVE
Holly

After a few days of initial chemotherapy and many more tests, Gwen is released from the hospital but needing to return in two weeks for what is called induction chemotherapy. She will stay in the hospital for a week or two and then, depending on her blood work, should be able to come home. I've never seen Gwen like this before. Gwen is usually so strong, so chill and funny. She's easygoing and full of life. Now her skin is a ghostly white, her eyes have dark circles around them and her ever-present smile has faded. Mom tells me that Gwen is going to stay at our house for a little while. That way she can help her out at home and keep an eye on her.

Mom and I go to Gwen's apartment to pick up some of her things to make the guest room feel more like it's hers. Mom drops me back off at home before leaving for the hospital to bring Gwen back. She tells me that she doesn't want to overwhelm Gwen and puts me in charge of cooking dinner. I veto cooking and order pizza. While I wait for the pizza, I head into Mom's office looking for an extra notebook. I'm searching through her desk drawers when I hear Mom and Gwen come in through the garage. They are talking in the laundry room, which is right beside her office. I hear their muffled tones through the wall; they both sound serious. I tip-toe out into the hallway and stand up against the wall where they can't see me.

"Gwen," Mom's voice sounds strained. "I can't keep arguing about this with you."

"Then don't," Gwen's voice has a tone that I've never heard before. She sounds aggressive and domineering.

"You heard what Dr. Anderson said. If the chemo doesn't work you'll need a –."

"I know what she said. Look, I don't want to keep doing this. What's done is done, let's just stop bringing it up."

"You need to tell Holly, Gwen," I can hear the shakiness in Mom's voice. She sounds afraid. I've never heard her sound like this before. What is going on?

"I can't," Gwen whispers.

I sigh. I've had enough of these secrets. I'm so tired of the two of them and all the things that they feel the need to hide from me. I come out from around the corner. "Tell me what?" I ask. I watch as Mom's eyes go wide and Gwen turns around to face me. Neither of them says anything. They just stand there staring at me. "Tell me what?" I ask again. Mom puts a heavy hand on Gwen's shoulder.

Gwen takes a shaky breath. She doesn't speak. She is staring at me like I have some kind of disease. Then finally words come out of her mouth.

"Let's go into the living room," she says. Mom walks over to me, she takes my hand and leads me to the couch. The three of us sit down. I'm in between Mom and Gwen. I feel something strange shift between the three of us, it's almost like Mom is trying to protect me from Gwen. She's still holding my hand. My mom isn't an overly affectionate person, so this is slightly weird and uncharacteristic.

Gwen looks paler than pale. Her normally olive tanned skin looks pasty and sweat covered. Her lips are dry and I can see she's breathing very quickly. We sit there for what seems like forever.

"So is anyone going to tell me what they need to tell me or are we just going to sit here all night?" I'm reaching a new level of annoyance. Mom and Gwen are looking at each other. It's like they are talking with their eyes.

"This is really difficult," Gwen begins. "I don't know where to start."

"Start at the beginning," Mom says in a soft voice. I'm now beyond confused. I thought they were going to talk to me about Gwen's cancer, but by the way they are both acting it seems like something entirely different.

"Holly, you already know some of this story," Gwen's voice quivers as she speaks. "Katie and I were eighteen when your grandparents passed away and their death – well, lets just say it really took a toll on me. I left our town and went off to college but I was in a very dark place. I found comfort in drugs and alcohol and men. I went on benders for days at a time. I honestly don't even know how I didn't get kicked out of school. When I was twenty-one, I was at a party one night. I wasn't doing drugs anymore, but I was still drinking heavily. I was wasted at this party, Holly. I wish I could say I remembered more from that night, but I don't. I hooked up with one of my old boyfriends at the party. That was the last time I ever saw him again."

Gwen pauses for a minute. Mom gets up and walks over to the kitchen. She gets a glass of water and brings it back over to Gwen.

"Thanks." Gwen takes a few small sips of water. "A month later I found out I was pregnant."

Pregnant. This had not been the story that I was expecting. So somewhere out there I had a cousin?

"I stopped drinking right away," Gwen says quickly. "I decided that I was going to keep the baby and raise it on my own. I could stay in school. People do it all the time."

"Like my mom," I say.

Gwen swallows hard. "Like your mom." Her voice cracks.

Suddenly it clicks in my mind. I realize what Gwen is trying to tell me and I gasp. On my left side, Mom squeezes my hand.

"I had a relatively easy pregnancy," Gwen continues. "I was pretty sick at the beginning of it, but I think some of it was probably my body detoxing as well. I stayed in school and then nine months later, I gave birth to a beautiful baby girl. A few weeks later I began to panic. I didn't know how to be a parent. I'd just given birth to a child and was all by myself. I felt worthless and old thoughts began to creep back into my mind. Old habits started to creep up again." I wondered what that meant, but I was too paralyzed to ask. I think I've only heard about 50% of everything that she has been saying to me. "So I took the baby –."

"Me," I whisper. "You took me."

"Yes." Tears are streaming down Gwen's cheeks. "I took you to my sister. To Katie. I knew that Kate would know what to do. I knew that she would be able to take care of you and provide for you in ways that I couldn't. So I brought you to Kate." She stops. "To your mom."

My mind is spinning at one hundred miles per hour. I don't know if I want to laugh, cry or punch someone in the face. I'm not really sure how to comprehend all of this. My breathing feels shallow. I feel my face getting really hot. The doorbell rings. Gwen makes a confused face and Mom frowns. Mom gets up off the couch and walks through the kitchen and into the foyer to answer the door. I hear her talking; she comes back to the kitchen and gets her purse. The pizza. A few minutes later she brings the pizza box and three plates over to the couch and puts the box on the coffee table.

"What are you thinking, Holly?" Mom asks as she sits back down beside me. I shrug. All my emotions are a whirlwind. Shrugging is the best I can do.

"What happened next?" I ask. I don't look at Gwen.

"Next," Gwen says. She puts her hand lightly on my arm and I jump. She pulls back for a second and then puts her hand back down on my skin. "I left you with Kate and I went back to school. I went back into a very dark place." She kept saying this like I was supposed to know what it meant. My face must have shown what I was thinking because she elaborated. "I became very depressed. I dropped out of school for a semester. I didn't leave my apartment. I didn't talk to anyone. It took months for me to start working through everything that had happened. We can talk about that more another time."

My mom wasn't really my mom. She was my aunt. Gwen was my mom. Why the hell had they both lied to me all these years? There were things that made so much sense now. Why I had always felt so close with Gwen. Why Gwen and I looked so alike when Mom and I didn't. My brain felt like it could explode. My heart was racing.

"Holly?" Gwen is looking at me. She looks so tired.

"I don't understand," I say. "So you just gave me up? To her?" I put a strong emphasis on the word her and it comes out sounding a lot worse than intended. I see a hurt look form on Mom's face. I should care, but I don't. They have both lied to me for the past sixteen years.

"I did what I thought was best at the time," Gwen explains.

"But you came back," I say. "Why did you come back? Did you want me back?"

"Sweetie," Gwen says, and I cut her off.

"Don't call me that." My voice fills with a rage I don't recognize.

"Sorry," Gwen looks taken back. She looks like she doesn't know what to say.

"It was never a matter of Gwen not wanting you," Mom says. "Gwen did what she thought was best for you. You staying with Gwen wouldn't have been good for you."

"But why lie about it?" I cry. "Why did you say you were my mom?"

Mom sighs a sad, concerned sigh. "You started calling me mama as soon as you could talk. I tried to correct you but you didn't understand. I had legal adoption papers drawn up and mailed to Gwen. She signed them and sent them back. Legally you are my daughter."

"Why would you do that? She's your sister." I'm confused.

Now it's Gwen's turn to talk. "I was a mess babe –err – Holly. She needed to make sure you were safe. She did it for you. It was the right thing to do."

"You still didn't tell me why you came back."

"I wanted to know you," Gwen said. "I wanted to see you grow up, to be a part of your life. That night that I showed up in Fife Springs, I had no idea if your mom would even let me see you. Thankfully she did. I'm so grateful for that and for all of the time we've gotten to spend together since then."

"But it's all been based on a lie." I'm starting to feel more and more angry. My whole life, everything that I thought I knew wasn't real.

"It doesn't change anything," Mom reaches out for me. I pull back.

"It changes everything," I stand up. "I can't handle this. I need to go."

"Holly," Mom stands up.

"Let her go," Gwen says.

"What?" I stare at her like she's grown a double head. Gwen was never one to let me walk away from a conversation between us.

"Go cool off. Go process. I need to go lay down." She puts her hand to her head like she's balancing her body. She looks even worse than before. "We can talk more later. I'm sure you'll have more questions. I'll answer whatever you want me to. I just really need to go rest for a bit." I almost feel sorry for her. Almost.

Gwen stands up and walks towards the stairs. There's something about her walking away from me again that makes me feel like I'm going to lose my mind. I know she's sick but the two images aren't correlating in my brain. I walk towards the front door, tear my coat forcefully off the coat rack and walk outside, slamming the door behind me. I stand on the front porch and begin to cry. I cry and cry and cry. I feel so alone. So lost. My entire life I had been told a lie. I wonder if I'll ever feel whole again.

THIRTEEN
Gwen

I am numb. I drag my body up the stairs into Kate's guestroom. I sit down on the bed and try to focus on my breathing. Everything feels heavy. I'd carried this secret for so long that you would think I'd feel better now that everything was out on the table. I didn't. Everything in me wanted to run away. I was terrified. I saw the look in Holly's eyes. She hated me. She thought I was disgusting.

After a few minutes, Kate knocks on the door and comes into the room. She sits down on the bed beside me.

"How is she?" I ask.

Kate looks at me with sad eyes. "I don't know. She left."

"You didn't go after her?"

"No," Kate says. "She needs time. I'm sure she is furious with me too."

"She hates me." I look down at my hands.

"Do you think we did the right thing?" Kate asks.

"I hope so." The room is starting to spin and I'm feeling nauseous. I'm not sure if it's from the chemo or the events of the evening. I put both my hands down on the comforter to brace myself.

"Are you okay?" Kate looks at me with concern. I nod. "You?"

"Not really," she shrugs. "Saying all of that aloud for the first time in years...it brought up some old stuff."

"Me too."

"Do you mind if I tell Duane?" Kate turns to face me.

"I'm surprised you haven't already." I take a deep breath. The nausea lets up a bit.

"I thought you'd slay me if I did." Kate nudges me. I give her a small smile in response.

"So an old boyfriend?" Kate looks me in the eyes. "Was it Christopher? Alex?"

I shake my head. "Not right now. I'm going to lay down for a bit."

"Seriously?" she grumbles. "You still aren't going to tell me who her dad is?"

"I think I should tell her first. I'm surprised she didn't ask."

"She's probably in shock." Kate moves and hugs me quickly. "It's going to be okay," she whispers into my hair. She strokes my back for a minute and helps me get into bed. Leave it to Kate to be the little sister who always picks up the pieces for her big sister. After she leaves, I stare at the ceiling. I wonder how I'm going to do this. Leukemia and Holly. I'm so tired. I feel my brain start to shut off as sleep takes over, and I'm left wondering if any of this has been worth it.

FOURTEEN
Kate

I slip out of the guest room and make my way downstairs to the living room. I see the unopened pizza box on the coffee table and my stomach grumbles. I can't remember the last time I ate. I open the box and am hit with the aroma of delicious pizza. I pick up a slice and take a bite. It tastes just as good as it smells. My cell phone rings, of course. I put down the slice and answer. "Kate Sherwood."

"Hi Kate, it's Tracy Anderson."

"Oh, hi Tracy." Panic spreads through my body.

"I just wanted to let you know Holly is here. I told her I'd give you a call and let you know I'd bring her home later."

"Okay, thanks," I say.

"No problem," her voice is soft and sounds concerned.

"Tracy?"

"Yes?"

"How does she seem?"

"She's upset," Tracy says in a low voice. "She didn't say why. I'm assuming it has to do with Gwen's diagnosis. It can be so difficult to see someone you love so sick. She just asked if she could stay here."

"Thank you," I say quietly. I hadn't thought about what airing our dirty laundry would be like. Like most small towns, nothing in Fife Springs was ever kept quiet for too long. If Holly told Griffin, I could only assume it would be a matter of time before more and more people began to find out.

This was one of the reasons why I had made sure every I was dotted and T was crossed when it came to Holly. I knew that one day people would find out what Gwen and I had done and, morally, I knew that it could have repercussions on my career. I felt a wave of guilt over what Gwen had told Holly before – that I'd done what I'd done to protect her. That was true, but I'd also done it to protect myself. I couldn't bear the thought of Gwen coming back and taking Holly from me. It would have torn me apart in a million ways. Holly was my all, my everything; without her, I would be nothing.

I called Duane and asked if he could come over. I was anxious about telling him the truth. I didn't know how he would respond. Would he be hurt? Would he be angry? I'd lied to him to. All of me prayed that he would be able to understand why I didn't tell him the truth about Holly.

I'd eaten half a pizza by the time Duane showed up. He immediately helped himself to some pizza and sat down on the couch with me. I think I would have to burn this couch if I had to share any more bad news on it. "How's Gwen?" he asks me between bites of pizza.

"She's okay," I snuggle up beside him. "The chemo is really tiring her out. She's sleeping right now. I have to tell you something."

"Oh yeah?" He grins at me and kisses my head. "What's that?"

"It's serious."

"How serious?" He kisses me on the mouth.

"Duane!"

"Okay, okay," he wraps his arms around me. "What's up?"

"Gwen's cancer…it's brought up some things." I sound like a crazy person. I don't know what to say. So I start at the beginning. I tell him everything. I tell him about my parents dying, about Gwen going off the rails, about her showing up on my doorstep right before Christmas just over sixteen years ago. I tell him things that Holly doesn't even know yet. About Gwen getting smashed the night before she decided to bring Holly to me. About her leaving Holly alone for hours. When I finally stop talking, Duane doesn't speak right away.

"Duane?" I say. "Are you mad?"

He shakes his head. "Sorry, this is just a lot to take in."

"I know," I say. "I'm so sorry I didn't tell you, but I couldn't."

"I get it," he looks shaken. "Gwen is your sister. Your loyalty was to her."

"But you're mad…"

"I'm not mad…" He sits up straighter on the couch. "I'm just hurt. But I get it. I get why you couldn't tell me when Holly didn't know. I understand that it was Gwen's secret too. I just can't help but wonder what it will be like when we get married one day."

I swallow hard. "What do you mean?"

"Are you always going to go to Gwen first? Is she always going to be your person over me?"

"That's not fair," I argue.

"Maybe not," Duane sighs. "I just need to process all of this."

"What does that mean?" My heart is racing.

"It means that I love you and I've had a really long day. I need to go get some sleep and we can talk more tomorrow." He hugs me and my eyes fill with tears. I honestly had never thought that Duane would have an issue with everything that Gwen and I had done.

"Okay," I whisper. Duane lets go of me and sees my glazed over eyes.

"Hey, don't cry," he tells me. "It's okay." I walk him to the door and say goodnight. I go back to the couch and polish off the rest of the pizza. I text Holly to ask her when she's coming home. She doesn't respond. I curl up in a ball on the couch, close my eyes and wonder when the hell things got so complicated.

FIFTEEN
Holly

The ten-minute walk to Griffin's house is cold. I get to his front door and realize I'm shivering. I ring the doorbell and Griffin's mom answers. I don't even know if he's home. I haven't told him I'm coming over.

"Holly!" Dr. Anderson smiles at me.

"Hi, Dr. Anderson," my voice is shaky and I can feel my eyes wet with tears.

"Oh honey, call me Tracy," she smiles at me. "Is everything okay, Holly?" She looks at me with genuine parental concern and sympathy.

"Yeah," I say. "I'm just having a bad day. Is it okay if I hang out here for a bit?"

"Of course! Griffin's upstairs." She motions me to come inside the house. "Griffin!" She calls. "Holly's here!"

Ten seconds later Griffin pounces down the stairs. "Hey babe," he says, wrapping me in a hug. "What's wrong?"

"Nothing," I say. "I'm just tired."

"Do you want to stay for dinner, Holly?" Dr. Anderson asks. "John should be home soon." John is Griffin's dad. He runs a car dealership in town.

"I already ate," I lie. I'm not the least bit hungry. "Thank you, though." Griffin leads me into the family room. His parents have even stricter rules than my mom. When we're at his house, we're only allowed on the main floor. The main floor is open concept so you can see everything from whatever room you're in.

"So what's wrong?" Griffin asks as we sit on his parent's pristine white couch. I think for a moment. I didn't really think things through before coming here. Suddenly I don't want to be here at all. I want to be at home in my bed sound asleep.

"Nothing," I say. "Just girl stuff, you know." He didn't. I felt a sense of loyalty towards my mom. I was so mad at Gwen and her for keeping this secret from me, but I knew that my mom prided herself on being graceful and composed. I knew what this secret would do to her. As hurt as I was, she was still the woman who had raised me. That had to count for something.

"You must be so worried about Gwen," he says, his dark eyes filled with concern. I nod slowly in response.

I just wanted to talk to someone I could trust, and right now that person wasn't Griffin. We'd barely been dating for more than five minutes. I didn't think he even knew my middle name. There was only one person I wanted to talk to right now and that person was Emma. My best friend who I had been ignoring for weeks – from hiding my relationship with Griffin to giving her the heist when Gwen was in hospital.

"Hey Griff," I say softly. "I'm sorry to do this, but do you think you could take me to Emma's house? I really need to talk to her."

If he looks hurt, he doesn't show it. "Of course," he tells me. He calls to his mom that he's driving me to Emma's and we leave.

We get to Emma's beautiful old Victorian-style house a few minutes later. Emma's house is my dream house. It's light blue with white trim and a massive wrap-around porch with two rocking chairs on in. Emma meets me on the porch. "Let's sit out here," she motions to the rocking chairs. Her house is comparable to a circus with her four siblings. You can hear the soft echo of laughter and noise coming from inside the house. Emma opens a wicker chest that sits between the rockers and hands me a warm fuzzy down blanket. She takes another one out for herself. "We can go in if it gets too cold. It's just quieter out here. So what's up? How's Gwen?"

"Gwen's my mom." I take a deep breath. Saying the words out loud makes me feel dizzy and also like I'm going to throw up.

"Huh?" Emma purses her lips and raises her eyebrows.

"You have to vault everything I'm about to tell you."

"Always."

"Gwen is my biological mom. Spark notes version, she was off the rails, got knocked up with me at a party, gave me to my mom when I was three weeks old and didn't see me again until she showed up here. So my mom is actually my aunt, and Gwen is actually my mom." I sound like a crazy person.

Emma doesn't say anything for a minute. I slowly rock my chair back and forth and listen to the soft creak. Finally she speaks. "That sounds like a bad Lifetime movie." She shakes her head. I burst out laughing. "Sorry," she says. "I'm not trying to be insensitive. But what the hell? Who springs that on you after sixteen years? Like what do they even expect you to do now?"

"I don't know," I clasp my hands together. "I'm so mad."

"Who are you mad at?" Emma looks at me with concern.

"I'm mad at Gwen. I can't even look at her, Em. I don't know what to say to her. She didn't want me."

"Do you really think that's true?" she asks in a gentle voice. "It sounds like she gave you to your mom because she wanted something better for you."

"I guess," I mutter. This is exactly why I had wanted to come talk to Emma, because she was very logical. A voice of reason.

"Don't get me wrong," she says. "I'd still be pissed, but to me, your mom is still your mom. She raised you, and she did an amazing job."

My eyes fill with tears. "I feel like I can't trust either of them."

"I think that will just take time, Holl. It's okay to be mad. I think it will just take small baby steps. You guys will figure it out." I nod in response. "What about your dad?" Emma asks.

I sigh. I hadn't even thought about that. I'd spent most of my life annoyed that my mom wouldn't give me any details about my birth father. Now I realized it was likely because she didn't know who he was. She should've just lied. "Gwen said he was an old boyfriend."

"Really?" Emma squints. "I wonder who he is. I wonder if he even knows about you."

"I wouldn't count on it." I feel deflated.

We talk for a while longer and by the end of our conversation, the heavy load on my chest feels a little bit lighter, but all I want is sleep.

Emma drops me off at home just after eleven o'clock. I'm exhausted. I tip toe in through the front door. The kitchen light is on and I see Mom asleep on the couch. I walk over to her and cover her up with a blanket. She doesn't even move. I'm mad at her, but I don't want her to freeze.

I turn off the kitchen light and move towards the stairs. When I get to the top of the stairs I see that the guestroom door is open and a small bit of light trickles from the room. I want to look, but I don't.

I walk past the door, and I know that Gwen is watching me. I feel a small sense of victory as I walk into my room and close the door behind me.

Sleep doesn't come. I toss and turn for hours. Finally I check my phone and see that it's four thirty in the morning. I do something uncharacteristic. I put on sweatpants and a long-sleeved thermal shirt. I lace up my running shoes and head outside. It's dark out. My mom would kill me if she knew I was out here. I exit out the front gate, and I break into a run.

I hate running, but it is my mom's lifeline. When I was younger, Mom used to drag me to the track with her and make me run laps. "It's good for your mind," she'd tell me. I was reluctant to believe her. My mom ran almost every day religiously, whereas I would rather take a nap. I run until I can't feel my legs and my ankles scream out in pain. I wheeze heavily. I make a mental note that I need to get in better shape. I slow down to a walk and make my way back home. It is freezing out, but my body feels warm. I watch as my breath turns white in the air.

For the first time in my life, I think that I finally understand why Mom runs. I feel a strange new sensation running throughout my entire body. I feel like I can do anything in this moment. My head feels clear and I feel less angry. I feel this new sense of empowerment – all this from a morning jog, wow. I'm almost home when I see tiny white snowflakes beginning to fall from the sky. I love snow. It's probably one of my most favourite things in the world. Everything is beautiful when it snows. It's fresh, symbolic almost. It reminds me of redemption, of being wiped clean.

I go in through the gate and sit down on the bench on the front porch. I watch as the flakes become heavier and start to stick to the ground. The front door opens and Mom walks outside. She is holding a blanket. She sits down beside me and drapes the blanket over both of our shoulders. She is quiet for a few minutes but her breathing is rapid and I can tell she's nervous.

"So you went for a run," she comments, glancing down at my runners.

I shrug. "I couldn't sleep."

"Sorry to hear that."

"Do you know what time it is?" I ask her.

"Around five thirty I think. I heard you leave." She shivers under the blanket.

"Ah," I frown.

"Can we go inside and talk? It's freezing out here."

I nod and stand up. I follow her into the house. I sit at the island and Mom pours me a steaming mug of something hot. I take a sip. It's my favourite hot chocolate that she always used to make me when I was little.

"When did you make this?" I ask.

"While you were out. I heard it was supposed to snow." Mom bites her lip. This is very uncharacteristic of her. My mother never looks uncertain. "Holly, I'm so sorry. I don't even think you can begin to understand how sorry I am. Last night – that's not how I wanted you to find out."

"How come you never told me?" I ask. I take another sip of my drink. The warm mug feels nice on my iceberg hands.

"I thought you would hate me," she confesses. "I mean, not that I'm doing so well in the Mom Department these days anyway. My plan had always been to tell you when you were old enough to understand – before Gwen ever showed up, but I was scared. More time passed. Then one day Gwen was on my doorstep and I was terrified that she had come to take you back. I love you so much, sweetheart. I know you're probably furious with me. I hope that one day you can understand why we did what we did and that you'll forgive me." I cringe at her use of the word we.

"I'm sick of all the lies," I say. My eyes begin to water and tears start to fall down my cheeks.

"Come here." Mom reaches over to me and tries to take my hand. I pull my hand away. I see her face fall, her lips forming into a sad frown. "I'm so sorry, Holly. I know you're hurting, and I wish I could fix it."

"I just feel like a huge part of me is empty," I tell her. Then I ask her what I've been wondering ever since Emma brought it up the night before. "Do you know who my dad is?"

"I don't," Mom admits. "I have a few ideas. I think that you should talk to Gwen about it."

I roll my eyes. "I don't want to talk to her about anything."

"I know." Mom's voice is quiet, almost a whisper. "But she might be able to give you some answers." Whatever. I glare at her in response. "I love you," she adds.

Out of spite, I don't return her affection. I can tell she wants to comfort me, but I'm not ready for that. I feel something different between us. Things have changed and it hurts so much.

"I'm going to go shower. Then I need to get organized for school tomorrow." Tomorrow was the first day of the new semester. I honestly didn't know how I was going to sit through a day of classes. This semester I had chemistry, P.E., English lit and a spare, so besides the chemistry it wasn't going to be too work-intensive.

Gwen ignores me for most of the day. I don't know what I'd been expecting, but I hadn't been expecting that. I see her in passing a few times. She looks awful, like she hasn't slept at all. Mom is at work, so it's just the two of us in the house. It's midafternoon when I go downstairs and she's in the kitchen drinking a glass of carrot juice that looks absolutely disgusting. I know she has chemo again tomorrow and will be in the hospital for most of the day.

I look at her, but she looks away. What the hell. I'm already on a short fuse. "Hi to you too," I mutter. I grab a glass from the cupboard, open the fridge and pour myself a glass of water.

"Hi," Gwen's voice is hollow and monotone.

"So what is your new plan, that you're just never going to talk to me again? Like that's some brilliant idea? Just, 'Hey Holly, I'm your mom,' and then nothing? Who does that? I don't get you at all. Normally you're pouncing on me to talk to you about everything and anything and now you won't even look at me? I don't even know why you're here. Maybe you just should've never come here."

I say the last words, and I know I don't mean them. Up until yesterday, Gwen was one of my favourite people. She was my cool aunt, my confidant, someone who I knew I could talk to without judgment. She was strong, she was smart and she was everything I wanted to be. Until now. Now she just looks weak to me. I don't wait for her to respond, I stomp out of the kitchen and back up the stairs to my room. I slam my door hard. It feels good to get angry.

My door opens and Gwen walks in. "Thanks for the knock," I say with thick sarcasm.

"Cool it," she snaps, which surprises me. Gwen isn't an angry person. "Sit," she motions to my bed. Her voice is firm and unwavering. I'm a bit taken back, but I do as she says. She sits down beside me. I'm expecting her to give this big speech but instead she says nothing.

"So are we just going to sit here or were you planning on saying something?"

"When did you become such a smart ass?" She groans and then shakes her head as if she's trying to clear her mind. "Look, I'm sorry if I made you feel…ignored? That wasn't my intent. I was just trying to give you some space. I wanted to let you think things over. Honestly Holly, for years I've wondered if you would ever speak to me again after you found this out. I know that I betrayed your trust, and I'm sorry."

"Okay," I reply. I don't know what else to say.

"You take all the time you need." Gwen pauses. She looks like she's thinking hard about her next words. "There's a reason why we told you this now."

I had wondered about that. When I had overheard Mom and Gwen talking, she had seemed adamant that I know now. Why?

"If my chemo doesn't work, my next best treatment option is a bone marrow transplant. Because you're my biological daughter there would be a chance that you would be compatible as a donor – your mom, too."

"So you want me to get tested? That's why you told me the truth?" I see Gwen's face change, and I know she's realized that she has brought this up at the wrong time.

"You know what? You said you wanted me to be honest, so I will be," Gwen bites her lip. "Yes, that's why I told you." My eyes widen. "Holly, if it were up to me I probably never would have told you the truth, but circumstances change."

I hate her so much right now. I feel anxiety begin to creep up in my mind. Never in my life have I felt so unwanted and alone. I hate her. "Go," I hiss the words out between my teeth in an icy tone that I don't even recognize.

She looks taken back. "Holly, I don't think you –."

"I don't want to talk to you anymore, Gwen," I put an emphasis on her first name. "Get out of my room." I pause. "Now." I can feel my breath getting short and my chest starts to feel heavy. She's watching me now, studying me very carefully. She looks concerned, but she gets up and leaves my room.

I sit on the edge of my bed and try to calm myself down, but I can't. I bundle myself up and go for a walk instead. Outside, the snow is still falling. It's still so beautiful and looks perfect, which is basically the opposite of how I'm feeling in this moment: battered and broken.

Forty-five minutes later, I end up at the courthouse. I'm freezing. I get inside and order a coffee from the coffee bar and then make my way to Mom's office. I'm surprised that she's in her office and not in court.

"Hi, sweetie." She stands to greet me, takes in the wrath of anger I bring into the room and walks over to me. "What's wrong?" She motions me to sit down in one of the two chairs in front of her desk. She doesn't try to hug me this time. She takes a seat beside me instead of behind her desk.

"I talked to Gwen this afternoon." I purse my lips in a tight line. I feel the rage begin to rise up in me just from saying her name.

Mom sighs. Her brown eyes look worn and tired, with dark circles under them. "What happened?"

"She basically told me that the only reason she told me the truth about being my mom." I stop midsentence and notice Mom's face pain a little at the words "my mom." "My biological mom," I stutter and shake my head. I don't know why I care about how she feels. She clearly didn't take my feelings into consideration over all of these years. "Was because she had cancer. She said that I might be compatible for a bone marrow donor."

"I'm sure she didn't mean it like that." Mom's voice sounds strained.

"I asked her if she meant she never would have told me and she said that she only told me because she had cancer." Rehashing this conversation brought all my anger back.

"Well, I don't think that's true." Mom sounds like she is carefully choosing her words. "Gwen would have told you one day. I know she would have. Do I think it would have been yesterday if she didn't have cancer? Probably not."

"Why are you defending her?" I ask. "You didn't even hear the way she sounded. She was so harsh. I don't know what her problem is. It's not my fault she was a druggy who ruined her life and got knocked up."

"Hey! Don't talk about Gwen that way." Her voice is firm. She puts her hands over her eyes like a tent and begins to rub her temples with her thumbs. "Sweetie, I'm not defending her. I'm just trying to understand how to make sense of all of this. Gwen is going through a really rough time right now. She's not herself. I know this isn't fair, and I understand that you're angry but you may need to give her a little bit of grace and time to figure some things out."

"Why doesn't anyone care about me and what I need?" I raise my voice to a yell. My hands are starting to shake.

"Holly." Mom takes a deep breath. "I understand that you're upset."

"Upset! I'm way past upset! I'm freaking pissed off," I scream. "I'm tired of this crap. You and Gwen and all your stupid secrets and never putting me first. I'm done!" I turn and storm out of her office. Then I run. I run out of the courthouse, I run down the main street through town. I'm aware that I'm acting like a child, but I'm too angry to care. I stop for no one and eventually end up at the end of Griffin's driveway. I walk up the driveway to the door and ring the doorbell. I plaster the biggest fake smile I can muster on my face. Griffin answers almost immediately.

"Hey babe," he smiles. "I didn't think you'd make it." Griffin's mom was working overnight and his dad was out of town. He'd invited a few friends over to kick off the new semester.

"Me neither," I say.

"Everyone's in the kitchen." He smiles, puts his arm around me and pulls me inside.

"Sounds good." I smile back.

We walk towards the kitchen together. A few of Griffin's friends are there, mostly guys and their girlfriends. I know Emma is planning on stopping by later. Music plays in the background, football is on TV, the kitchen island is loaded with snacks and I notice that a few of the guys have beers. This isn't uncommon for a high school party, although it surprises me a bit at Griffin's house. Griffin's parents are super strict and likely wouldn't be down with underage drinking in their house.

I mingle for a while, and then I'm bored. My mom has called me eight times since I left the courthouse. She texts me that she has a dinner meeting that she can't get out of and will try not to be too late but asks that I please call her back. I don't. I wander through Griffin's house. It's very elegant, with everything in its place. The décor is pristine, but not in a snobbish way.

I find my way to his bedroom. I've never been in Griffin's bedroom before. The walls are a dark navy blue. Two dark wooden bookshelves and a big oak desk line one wall. His queen-sized bed with a dark blue and green plaid comforter is on the other wall. His room is surprisingly clean for a teenage boy. The floor is spotless and there is just a jacket resting on his desk chair.

"What are you doing up here?"

I feel Griffin's arms go around my waist. I turn around to face him. "I just wanted to see your room."

"Oh yeah?" He grins at me.

"Yup." I smirk. He leans down, his tall frame over me and kisses me. The kiss is long and deep. I feel my mind begin to clear as I sink into the kiss. My shoulders start to relax and I feel comfort throughout my body. I just want to feel something different. I want to feel Griffin. In this moment I just want to be as close to him as I possibly can.

I don't know what comes over me. Suddenly I'm kissing him even harder, pulling at all parts of him. I feel out of control, yet in complete control at the same time. We kiss for a while longer, and we eventually find our way to his bed. I am trying so hard to forget about everything else that all I can focus on is Griffin and how I just want to feel close to someone. I stop for a second. "Do you have something?" I ask.

"I thought you were on the pill," he whispers.

"I am, but you know –."

"Hold on." He gets up and walks to the bathroom and comes back with a condom. I pull him towards me and get lost in his kiss once more.

When it's over, I feel terrible. Sex was not what I thought it was going to be like. I'd always thought that the first time I had sex, fireworks would explode, music would play, and that something would be different. If we're being completely honest, it was awkward and it hurt like hell. I feel embarrassed.

"Wow," Griffin says, when it's all over. "That was amazing."

"Yeah, amazing," I echo. I feel different but not in the way that I'd expected. I was looking for a satisfaction that I didn't receive. Actually, I just felt like an idiot. I don't know why I let myself get so caught up in a moment. We clean up and go back downstairs.

"Do you want something to drink?" Griffin asks.

"That would be great. Whatever you're having," I reply. He mixes me a drink and hands it to me. I don't usually drink. I got drunk once last year, spent the whole night puking at Emma's place and Mom found out and grounded me for a month. I take a sip of the drink. Whiskey and Coke. I just want to forget everything for one night. That shouldn't be too hard, right?

When Emma shows up an hour later, I'm completely smashed. "Emma!" I yell, throwing my arms around her.

"Oh God." She peels me off of her. "What the hell happened to you?"

"I just wanted to make it everything go away," I whisper. I grab a shot glass of the counter and fill it with tequila.

"Oookay, no more tequila for you." Emma looks concerned. She also looks blurry. Very blurry. I ignore her and take the shot. "Come with me." Emma links her arm through mine and leads me into what looks like someone's office. There's a desk, a couch and a few bookshelves. "Sit." I sit on the couch, but end up on the floor.

"I had sex with Griffin," I tell her. Then I start to cry. What happens next is very jumbled in my mind. I hear Emma talking, but I can't say anything to her. I just keep crying and crying. I feel so empty, so unloved and so very sleepy. I hear Emma say to come quickly and that she's never seen me like this before, but I don't think she's talking to me anymore. Then she wraps both her arms around me and hugs me tightly.

"It's okay, Holly," Emma says. "I love you. You're going to be okay."

I'm still crying when Gwen walks through the door. She's wearing yoga pants and an oversized cardigan. She looks better than she looked earlier. "What's she doing here?" I practically spit out the words. I'm not sure if my speech is coherent.

"Is Griffin here?" Gwen asks. Emma nods and points to the kitchen. Gwen leaves and comes back a few minutes later.

"I guess the party's over," Emma mutters.

"I called Tracy Anderson," Gwen tells her. "She's coming home. Have you been drinking?"

"No," Emma tells Gwen. "I just got here. I can get a ride home though."

"I'll drive you home. No one here is driving," Gwen says. She sounds pissed. I'm not used to seeing Gwen so angry. We wait for Griffin's mom. Gwen puts me in the car and I'm still a mess. Silent tears continue to fall from my face. Emma is sitting in the backseat.

"Why did you call her?" I ask, sobbing. "I don't want to see her."

"Holl, up until a few days ago you talked to Gwen about

everything. She was your favourite person. I called your mom first and she didn't answer, I didn't know what else to do." Emma leans forward between the two front seats and faces me. "Did he hurt you?" She asks.

I shake my head no. "I don't want to talk about it."

"You just don't seem okay." She puts her hand on my shoulder.

"I'm not."

She keeps her hand on my shoulder but leaves the conversation at that.

After what seems like forever, Gwen gets into the car. She doesn't say anything the entire car ride home, except goodbye to Emma when we drop her off. It's beginning to snow again and the roads are covered. I'm thinking about how pretty it looks when I'm overcome with a wave of nausea.

"I think I'm going to –," I throw the door open and puke half on the road, half inside her car.

"Lovely," she says sarcastically. A few minutes later she pulls into the driveway. She helps me out of the car and takes me into the kitchen, where she gets me some water.

Everything is spinning. Gwen helps me upstairs. She helps me change and puts me into my bed. "I'm such an idiot," I tell her. She sits down on the bed beside me and gently pushes a few strands of hair out of my face. "I don't know why I did it. I didn't want to sleep with him. I just wanted to feel something. I wanted to feel close to someone."

"Shhh," Gwen whispers, as she wipes the tears off my cheeks. "Go to sleep." I don't know how long she stays there. I don't remember her leaving but when I wake up in the morning she is gone, and I'm left feeling confused, carrying a heavy weight of emptiness.

SIXTEEN
Kate

After Holly storms out of my office I don't know what to do. Should I run after her? Should I give her space? I call Gwen instead. She answers on the first ring.

"What the hell is wrong with you?" I ask my sister.

"Hi to you too," she mumbles.

"Did you tell Holly that you never would have told her the truth if it wasn't for your cancer?" I'm fuming. I hate seeing Holly like this.

"Maybe." Gwen's voice is quiet. "She asked me to tell her the truth."

"Seriously, Gwen!" I groan. "You can't tell a sixteen-year-old that. She thinks you hate her."

"That's ridiculous, I don't hate her," I can almost hear Gwen roll her eyes through the phone. "I don't know what's wrong with me. It's like I've become completely inept when it comes to Holly."

"You need to talk to her, Gwen," I say. "I know you don't want to. I know it's easier to ignore it but you need to talk to her. She feels like you don't care about her because you gave her up. I know that's not true and so do you, but Holly needs to know too."

"I know," Gwen sighs. "Do you know what she's doing tonight?"

"No," I tell her. "I'll try calling her. She just stormed out of my office though, so I doubt she'll answer. I have a meeting with Judge Murray and the town council tonight. I'll try to be home as soon as I can but sometimes these meetings can drag on. School starts tomorrow too."

"Right," Gwen says. "I have chemo tomorrow morning." This was going to be Gwen's second round of inductive chemotherapy and she would be in the hospital for a few weeks. They were hoping that this would be successful and put her into remission. It was insane to me how fast this was all moving. I couldn't even begin to imagine how Gwen was feeling.

"I know. I'll drop you off."

"Thanks," she says. "I'll call you later."

"Okay. Bye" I hang up the phone. It rings almost instantly. I see Duane's name on the screen and answer immediately.

"Hi." I feel my chest begin to tighten.

"Hey beautiful," Duane's deep voice booms into the phone. "How's your day?"

"It was good up until about ten minutes ago." I fill him in on what happened with Gwen and Holly.

"That's rough," he says sympathetically. "Poor kid. I'd be a mess if I were her."

"Me too," I admit. "I just don't know what to do. Things have already been so rocky between us."

"You're still her mom," he says. "I'm sure she's pissed, but she's a teenager, she needs someone in her corner. Maybe you're not her mom biologically, but you raised her."

"True," I think about his words. He's right. I'm still her mom. This new dynamic is very confusing.

"Can we meet for dinner tonight?" He interrupts my thoughts.

"I can't do it tonight," I reply. "I have a dinner meeting and then a budget meeting after that. It's going to be a late night."

"Do you have time for coffee before?" He asks. I feel my heart rate start to speed up. Duane wouldn't break up with me over coffee, would he?

I glance at the clock on my wall. "I have an hour."

"Okay, meet me in ten then?"

"See you soon." I hang up the phone and pack up my things. I call Holly as I'm walking out of my office. She doesn't answer. I call again and it goes to voicemail after a few rings. Yup, she's pissed alright. I step outside and it's still snowing. This is strange for almost February in Fife Springs. I hug my coat tighter around my body. I get to the café and it's like a ghost town inside. Duane is already waiting for me at our usual table.

"I got you a coffee," he says. "I figured you'd need it for your long night."

"Thanks, I really appreciate it." I smile and give him a kiss on the cheek before sitting down. Duane was always taking care of me. Back when we had first met I had been doing things by myself for so long that I didn't think I needed anyone. It had taken me a long time to open myself up to Duane, to learn to trust him and be completely vulnerable around him.

"I just wanted to apologize for last night," he begins.

"What? Why? I'm the only who should be apologizing. I've been sick thinking about keeping that secret from you."

"Let me finish," Duane smiles. "I didn't mean to freak you out. I was just exhausted. This case I've been working on has me burning both ends of the candle. I understand why you couldn't tell me. I get that it wasn't entirely your secret to tell. If we're being honest though, part of me was hurt that you never told me, even though I completely understand why you couldn't."

I carefully sip my steaming hot coffee. "I get that. Honestly, Duane, there have been so many times that I've wanted to tell you. I'd even asked Gwen if I could tell you. We fought about it a lot. I wanted Gwen to tell Holly so long ago. I knew the longer that we waited the worse that it would be. It feels like this secret has slowly been killing me for years. Then yesterday when I realized that I could lose you, it just didn't seem like it had been worth keeping when it was just to protect Gwen."

"Well, and Holly," Duane says. He reaches across the table and takes my hand in his.

"But have I really been protecting her?" I ask him. "I think it might have just made things worse. She's convinced Gwen wants nothing to do with her. She thinks that she hates her. And I'm pretty sure I'm on the bottom of her list of favourite people."

"She's a teenager," Duane says softly. "It's going to take time."

"I keep reminding myself that." I make a pouty face.

"Can I take you out this weekend?" he asks. "On a real date?"

I grin. "Please! Gwen starts chemo again tomorrow, so she will be in the hospital for at least one week."

"I hope that she kicks cancer's ass."

"Me too." I look down at my watch. "I need to get going. Thanks for the coffee and the chat. I love you."

"I love you too, Katie." He stands up from the table, kisses me softly on the lips and pulls me into a hug. Duane still makes my knees weak.

I walk from the café back to the courthouse and drive over to the restaurant where I'm meeting Judge Murray. Wesley Murray was my mentor and a dear old friend of mine. He had taken me under his wing as a young lawyer and had been the one to recommend me for judgeship when the position became available. In many ways, he was like a father to me and had been like a grandfather to Holly over the years.

One of the reasons I'd asked to have a dinner meeting with him was to discuss everything that had conspired over the past few days. I wanted to be as transparent as possible. Wes had texted me saying that he was running a bit late. I call Holly three more times from the car and then text her saying I'm going to be in meetings but to call me back anyway. She doesn't respond. I'm starting to worry. I text Gwen asking if Holly is at home, she replies back saying she isn't and that she hasn't heard from her.

Despite my distraction over Holly, Wes and I have a nice dinner. I fill him in on everything that has happened. He reassures me that because I have taken the proper legal precautions that this really should be a non-issue in regards to my job. He warns me that people will talk, but at the end of the day my family business is just that and to take people's reactions with a grain of salt.

After dinner we drive over to our meeting in separate vehicles. About half an hour into our meeting I look down at my phone and see that I have a missed call from Emma Fields and a text from Gwen telling me to call her when I can. I excuse myself from the meeting and head out in the foyer area.

Gwen answers on the second ring. "Hey, I'm just going to get Holly. Emma called me. She said she tried you first but you didn't answer."

"I didn't hear my phone," I tell her. "Is Holly okay?"

"She's apparently very drunk and won't stop crying."

My heart breaks. "I can come, Gwen. I can meet you there."

"I got this." Gwen's voice is quiet. "I can do it. I'll pick her up and take her home."

"Do you know where she is?"

"At Griffin's." Gwen sighs heavily. "I already called his mom." Hearing those words I feel a sense of pride and also sadness. That was such a parental thing of Gwen to do. Gwen had never been much for rules when it came to Holly; she was just always available and ready to listen. The sadness came from a place of jealousy. I didn't want Holly to turn to Gwen as a parent; I wanted her to turn to me. I had raised her; she was my daughter. Then again, Emma had also tried calling me.

"Good," I tell her. "Okay, well if she's really not okay just tell me and I'll come home, okay?"

"I promise, I'll call if I need you. I have to go, I'm just pulling in." She hangs up the phone.

I stand very still and try to collect my thoughts before I go back inside. Part of me wants to say screw the meeting and go find Holly. Another part of me knows that I need to give Gwen some time with Holly to work through this new relationship. I know that they are going to have to figure it out together.

I was concerned that she'd been drinking. Actually, forget concerned – I was angry. Holly had only gotten drunk once and had sworn that she hated it and would never do it again. Granted, I wasn't that naive, I was more curious about what had caused her to do it and why. Had she wanted an escape? That made me nervous. Knowing Gwen's past with drugs and alcohol, I had always tried to be very open and honest with Holly about addiction. I didn't drink often; in fact, I typically only had a drink with Gwen or Duane. With my job, I was very cautious about how I was perceived in public and that meant that I almost never drank in social settings.

I feel a headache coming on. Most of my adult life I've been prone to migraines under stress. I rub my temples in a few circle motions and do the same to the pressure points between my thumb and index fingers. I put on my best professional face and walk back into the meeting room. For one of the first times in my career I feel completely done with my job and all it demands of my family and me. I just want to go home.

My meeting lasts another two hours. When I finally pull into my garage, it's well after ten and I'm exhausted. I'm almost scared to go inside, as I have no idea what awaits me. Gwen is sitting on the couch sipping something out of a mug.

"Hey," I call out to her.

"Hi." She turns and calls over her shoulder. I drop my pile of things on the floor, shuffle over to the couch and sit down.

"How are you feeling?"

"A lot better, actually. Nervous about tomorrow, though."

I nod. "Understandably. Is she asleep?"

"She is," Gwen looks reserved. I can't put my finger on it; she just looks like she doesn't want to be here with me.

"What happened?"

"I don't really know the whole story," Gwen sips her drink. "Emma called me. She told me that Holly was a drunken mess and that she wouldn't stop crying. When I got there she wasn't happy to see me. I waited for Tracy to get home and then drove Emma home, Holly puked in my car, I put her to bed and that was pretty much it. She was sloshed, Katie. I didn't think it was the right time for a heart to heart, not that she would have welcomed one from me anyway." Fair enough.

"She puked in your car." I make a face that shows my level of disgust. "I'll get her to clean it tomorrow."

"I already cleaned it," Gwen says. "It's fine, Katie. She was really upset. She's going to do stupid things sometimes. Hopefully not too stupid...but you know."

I can't help but feel like there's something she's not telling me, but I don't push it. "Well, thanks for picking her up...I really appreciate it."

Gwen nods in response.

"How was Tracy?" I ask.

"Furious," Gwen shakes her head. "His dad is out of down and she was working a double shift. Let's just say I think that Griffin's going to be grounded for a very long time."

"Yeah, well he can join the club with Holly. Nothing like being hung over on the first day of a new semester." I roll my eyes.

"Yeah." Gwen scrunches up her lips. "I don't think she's going to feel so hot in the morning."

"What time do you have to be at the hospital?"

"Eight thirty."

"Okay, I'll make sure Holly's up and we can drop her off on our way. I need to go to bed, I'm wiped."

"I should too."

We both stand up and I put my arm around Gwen's waist. Together we walk up the stairs and stop in front of the guest room. I give her a quick hug and tell her I'll see her in the morning. I head down the hall and pop into Holly's room. She's sound asleep. Then I retreat to my own room, craving my warm bed and a good night's sleep.

SEVENTEEN
Holly

I open my eyes and see that I'm in my bed. I'm confused. I try to sit up but am pulled back down by a pounding headache. I grab my phone, ignore the screen full of messages and see that it's only six. I put my head back down on my pillow and slowly begin to piece together the night before. I think back to my fight with Gwen, storming out on Mom, going to Griffin's. A sinking feeling hits my stomach when I remember the rest. My mind replays having sex with Griffin, followed by getting completely hammered. I remembered Gwen coming to get me. I don't remember what she said to me. I try to think hard but my brain feels fuzzy. I need water and a painkiller stat.

I slowly get out of bed and make my way downstairs to the kitchen. I'm surprised that no one else is there. I have some water and Tylenol and make a pot of coffee. I think about eating and decide to try a piece of toast. I'm just about to take my first bite when Gwen comes downstairs.

"Good morning." She nods at me.

"Morning." I shove a large bite of the toast in my mouth to keep it full.

"Feeling okay?" she asks.

"Headache," I mumble with a mouth full of bread. I swallow and a memory hits me. "Oh shit! Your car."

"Don't say shit," Gwen corrects me.

"Sorry. I can go clean it."

"I already did it."

"Okay. Thanks."

She doesn't say anything else. She makes herself some tea and sits down beside me at the island. I wish I could remember more of what happened. Had I said something to her? Had I told her about Griffin? My heart was pounding.

Mom walks in through the foyer in her running gear. "This whole snow thing is starting to get old," she says, peeling off a layer of clothing.

"It's coming down out there," Gwen agrees.

"I'm surprised you're awake," Mom remarks dryly.

"Headache," I tell her, and take a sip of coffee. I cringe at the bitter taste. I really don't know how people like this stuff.

"Well, from what I heard about last night that's not a surprise."

What did she hear? Ugh, this was driving me insane. "I don't really remember anything," I say to no one in particular. I watch Gwen who looks like she is contemplating something.

"This better not be a new thing." Mom pours herself a cup of coffee. "You know how I feel about you drinking."

"I know," I sigh. "I'm sorry. I don't really want to talk about it. It was stupid."

"I'm glad you've already realized that," Mom tells me. I can tell she is less than impressed. "It makes my job a lot easier. Grounded. One week, no phone, TV or internet at home – except for school work."

She let me off easier than I thought. "That's fine," I say.

"Oh is it fine?" She repeats like word like my response was venom. "The next time that you're angry, find a more appropriate way to express yourself. Hit a punching bag, go for a run, whatever. Understood?"

"Yes," I whisper. I can feel my eyes beginning to brim with tears. Mom goes upstairs to shower and I stare at my half-eaten toast, trying not to cry.

"Are you okay?" Gwen turns her head to look at my sideways face.

I continue to stare down. I can't reply without losing it so I just shake my head. I'm not really sure if my shake was a yes or no. I turn my face away from her entirely so that she can't see me.

"If you ever need to talk, you know I'm here," Gwen sounds like her old self. Like my fun, favourite, best listener in the world Aunt Gwen. I almost crumble, but I don't.

"Whatever," I mutter. I take another bite of my toast.

"Will you come see me when I'm in the hospital?" she asks. I notice the uneasiness in her voice. "Maybe we can talk more?"

"I'll think about it," I tell her. A single tear rolls down my cheek and I brush it off my face. I have so many questions I want to ask her, but half of me is still fighting the urge not to punch her in the face. "I'm going to go get ready for school."

I get to the top of the stairs and see Mom coming out of her room. She's wearing a bathrobe and has a towel on top of her head. I dart my eyes down to the floor so that she can't see the tears in them. I turn away from her and she calls after me, but I don't respond. Tears fall down my cheeks as I walk towards my room.

"We're leaving in twenty minutes," I hear her call as I close the door behind me.

I get dressed with practically zero effort. I pull my hair up into a bun, put on some black joggers, a black t-shirt and a black oversized sweater. I stare at my reflection in the bathroom mirror. I always thought that I would look different after having sex for the first time. Instead I just look like a train wreck. I have dark circles under my eyes and my usually tan skin looks lifeless. Too bad I don't care enough to bother with make up.

I grab my school bag from beside my desk and start to run down the stairs. Then I realize how hungover I am and my jog slows to a crawl.

"Whose funeral?" Mom asks, eying my choice of wardrobe as we walk into the garage.

"Mine," I mutter. She doesn't hear me because she's already getting into the car, but Gwen does. At least I think she does. She grabs my hand, looks directly into my eyes and squeezes my hand. That's when I remember. I told her about Griffin. My eyes go wide and she responds by giving me a sad smile. A part of me suddenly wants to tell her everything, a very small part. I want to forget about everything that's happened between us just for a few minutes so that I can tell her about what happened with Griffin. She lets go of my hand before I even have time to pull away from her.

I feel uncomfortable and like I should say something, but I don't. I walk over to the car and climb into the backseat. I watch as Gwen gets into the passenger seat. She looks sad. My heart aches. I can relate. I'm just not ready to talk to her yet.

I'm dreading school. Mom and Gwen drop me off first. I need to find Emma. I have chemistry first period. Emma doesn't take chem. Unfortunately, I don't have enough time to look for her. I sneak into the lab and sit in the back. I look down at my desk, praying that someone will sit down beside me before Griffin walks into the room.

"Hey babe." I hear Griffin's soft, husky voice beside me. I close my eyes and hear him pull out the chair next to me and sit down.

"Hi." My eyes are still closed. He kisses me on the cheek. I make a mental note not to wince.

"How are you feeling?"

"Headache."

"Can I get you anything?"

"I'm good, thanks." I don't know what's wrong with me. Shouldn't most girls who have sex with their boyfriend for the first time feel happy? I don't. I feel hollow and disconnected from him, even more than before. I had just wanted it to be something special, and it wasn't. I was angry at myself for using him to try and make me feel better in the heat of the moment; I was even angrier than it hadn't worked.

"Was Gwen pissed? Did she tell your mom? I'm grounded for a month. I guess there's a first and last time for everything." I knew he was referring to the party.

"Yeah. I'm grounded for a week. No cell phone, internet or TV at home."

"A week isn't bad...you got off pretty easy." Yeah, easy considering my mom and my aunt have been lying to me my whole life, and now my biological mom is going to be in the hospital because she has cancer. Sounds easy to me. It was probably a wise choice that I chose not to verbalize those thoughts. "So I guess we won't be seeing each other outside of school for a while," Griffin continues. His dark brown eyes sparkle. "I guess we'll need to find some time to hang out inside of school." He winks at me and drapes his arm loosely over the back of my chair.

"I guess so." My response is lame and sounds unexcited, but I just want to get out of here and talk to Emma. Thankfully the bell rings and our teacher walks into the room to start our class. When the bell rings signaling the end of class, I book it out of the classroom faster than a cat running away from a dog. I hear Griffin call after me but bolt to the girls' locker room to change for gym class. I know he won't be able to find me in here.

I sit on one of the benches in the change room. The walls are lined with navy blue lockers and the floor is tiled in medium-sized light grey squares. The benches are painted a dark grainy grey. Emma walks in a minute later. She sits down next to me and gives me a sideways hug.

"How are you?" she asks.

"A mess."

"So what the hell happened last night?"

The change room starts to fill with girls who are getting ready for gym class. "Not here," I tell her. We quickly get changed and exit the change room into the large gymnasium. We have Ms. Schiller for gym. She's a young fitness buff who we had last year. She's pretty chill and lots of fun. She tells us we are going to be doing fitness testing for the next two days to kick off the semester. Super.

Emma and I go outside to start with our timed mile run. We get to the track and decide to walk a lap to warm up. The snow has stopped and the track is clear, although the football field in the middle is a big white sheet. I hug my sweatshirt to my body and pull my hood up over my ears. "Now tell me," Emma says, when we are far enough away from anyone to be heard.

"Gwen and I got into a fight yesterday. She told me that she never would have told me about the switch if she didn't have cancer. Then I went to talk to Mom and we got into a fight. I was just so angry. I don't know how to process all of this. Then I ended up at Griffin's house."

"Where you had sex," she interrupts.

"Yes."

"How was it?"

"Honestly? Terrible. I wanted to wait. I just...I felt so numb. I wanted to feel something and I thought that it would help. It just made me feel worse. Now I don't know what to do. I can't even look at him."

"Sex doesn't have to big this big emotional thing," Emma tells me. "Sometimes it can just be fun."

"Not for me," I say, quietly. Emma lost her virginity when she was fourteen at a party and hasn't looked back since. "I've always wanted to it mean something."

"Fair enough." She starts jogging and I follow her lead. "So that's why you got completely sloshed."

"I guess that and everything else."

"What happened with Gwen?" Emma is in far better shape than me and I struggle to keep up with her.

"Oh you know, I puked in her car and told her I had sex."

Emma laughs. "What did she say?"

"I can't remember. She didn't say anything about it this morning. She asked if I would come visit her in the hospital."

"Are you going to?"

"I think so. I miss her. I'm so mad at her, but I miss her so much." I know it had only been a few days since Gwen and I had really talked, but because of how close we are it felt like an eternity to me. I can feel fill my eyes filling with tears. "I can't talk anymore, Em, I need to breathe." She laughs and we keep running. We clock in at a eight-and-a-half-minute mile, which isn't terrible considering neither of us are big runners and I'm extremely hung-over.

"I think you should go talk to Gwen," Emma tells me once we are back in the gym and about to complete a timed round of pushups. "I'll drive you this afternoon if you want. We have our spare last block and I'm on after-school pick-up duty."

"She might not be up for visitors today." I bite my lip. "Last time her first day of chemo was rough."

"Text her at lunch and ask."

"Okay." I take a deep breath. "Let's get this over with. Go." I hit my timer and watch Emma crush her pushups.

After many grueling rounds of core body exercises, my hangover headache was sticking around with full vengeance. Back in the change room, Emma pulls a sport drink out of her gym locker and hands it to me. "Drink this," she says. "You're probably dehydrated."

"Thanks." I take the bottle from her, twist off the cap and take a long sip.

"Text Gwen," Emma tells me.

"I don't know if I can."

"Sure you can." She picks up my phone and hands it to me. I type a message.

HOLLY: You up for a visit this afternoon?

Then I wait. We change together and then start to walk to our lockers. My phone buzzes; I pull it out and look at the screen.

GWEN: Yes. Come save me.

I almost smile. Almost.

"She said to come," I say to Emma.

"Good," Emma replies. "You need to be open minded when you talk to her. I know it's hard. I know you're angry, upset, betrayed – all of the above, but please Holly, just try to talk to her.

She's going to be in your life forever; she's your family." Emma was right. I knew she was right but it didn't make it any easier.

Emma and I go off campus for lunch. She lets me avoid Griffin because I've agreed to attempt at making peace with Gwen. One step at a time, she tells me. After English, we get into Emma's parents minivan and she drives me to the hospital.

"Want me to come inside?" she asks as we pull up to the main entrance.

"I think I'll be okay. Thanks though." I get out of the van and walk towards the main entrance, through the glass doors and then look around the main lobby of the hospital. There are armchairs on each side, a coffee shop, a gift shop and the main desk. I pass the main desk and go towards the elevators. I go two floors up to the Oncology unit. I walk through another set of glass doors and find the front desk.

A young male nurse, who looks overworked, is sitting at the desk. "Hi," I say. "I'm looking for Gwen Sherwood."

"One sec." He clicks a few things on the computer. "Room seven, take a right and it's your first left."

"Thanks," I nod my head at him and continue in the direction that he said. I get to room seven a minute later. The door is slightly ajar. I knock twice and go in.

Gwen is lying in a hospital bed in the middle of the room. She's hooked up to a few different machines that look scary to me. I'm surprised to see her sitting in bed reading a book. She sees me and smiles. "Hi!" she says. She looks tired and sick, sporting her new look of signature dark circles and pasty pale skin.

I shuffle closer to her bed. "Hey."

"You can sit," she motions to the chair beside her bed. I sit down. "How are you feeling?"

"Shouldn't I be asking you that?"

"I feel like I have no energy and am slightly nauseous. Your turn." She sounds like her old self.

"Same."

She laughs. "I'm glad you came."

"Emma said I should."

"Thank her for me," Gwen says. Then there's silence. Awkward, uncomfortable silence.

"I just wanted to talk to you about something." I tap my foot on the floor.

"About Griffin," she says in a knowing but gentle tone.

"Yeah...him...that," I frown. "Can we take a time out? I'm still really mad at you and I'm not ready to talk about all of that other stuff yet, but I need to talk to someone. I just...I can't talk to my mom about this. I just need to talk to my cool Aunt Gwen. So can you just be her for the sake of this conversation?"

Gwen doesn't say anything right away. She looks like she's thinking very carefully about what to say. "We're going to have to talk about the other stuff eventually."

"I know," I agree. "I'm just not ready yet."

Gwen nods. "Okay. Tell me about last night."

"Well you already know."

Gwen raises her eyebrows at me. "I know a slur of drunken words you mumbled to me as your head was hitting your pillow. That doesn't mean much." Point taken.

"After we talked yesterday, I went and talked to Mom and I got pretty mad. Then I went to Griffin's house. There were a few people from school there, just a back-to-school thing. I got bored waiting for Emma to get there and was hanging out in Griffin's room. I was pretty upset. Griffin came in and one thing led to another." I stop talking.

Gwen stares at me. "What exactly does that mean?"

"We had sex." I say the words and get that pit feeling in my stomach again. I close my eyes. I don't know what else to say. It's quiet for a couple of minutes and then I speak again. "Aren't you going to say something?"

Gwen purses her lips. "Were you safe?"

I nod. "I've been taking the pill since I got it, and I made him use a condom."

"Did he hurt you?"

"What?" I narrow my eyes. "You mean did it hurt?"

"No..." Gwen shakes her head. "Did he make you do anything you didn't want to do?"

"Oh, no."

"Okay." Gwen looks confused. "And you weren't drunk?"

"No, not then."

"Good," she says.

"Good?"

"Sorry." She shakes her head. "Honestly, this is new territory, even for me. I'm not used to the idea of you having sex."

"You aren't going to lecture me?" I start playing with a loose thread hanging off one of the bed sheets.

"I thought you weren't looking for a lecture."

"I'm not…"

"So what's wrong?" Gwen reaches out and puts her hands on my chin and gently lifts it up so that I'm looking at her again.

"I just…I wish I hadn't done it. Not like that anyway."

"Like what?" Gwen's tone is friendly and not judgmental.

"I always thought the first time I had sex it would be special…and it just wasn't. After it happened I just felt worse than I did before. I thought that it would make me feel better to be close with Griffin in that way. I just wanted to feel something different…now all I feel is regret."

"I'm sorry, babe." Gwen rests her hand on mine. "Sometimes in life we make mistakes, and that's okay. We learn from mistakes. They keep us grounded and they teach us lessons. I believe that if we handle them the right way, we come full circle and they eventually make us whole again and a hell of a lot stronger. I've made a lot of mistakes in my life. I wish I could tell you it gets easier but it doesn't. The most important thing you can do is forgive yourself and if you don't like the way that something happened make sure it doesn't happen again."

I'm hearing her words: *"I've made a lot of mistakes in my life."*

She must be a mind reader because she keeps talking. "You were never a mistake, Holly. You were the result of one, yes. But you yourself are one of the greatest blessings in my life. I hope you know that. Even though our family tree is a little bit broken and things in my life didn't turn out the way that I'd imagined they would. I need you to know that I've never thought of you as a mistake. In some of my darkest days, knowing that you were a part of me was what kept me going and made me better. I need you to know that."

"I do," I whisper. "I know now." A broken family tree. Her analogy kind of fit, as depressing as it sounded.

"Good." She takes my hand. "If you don't want to have sex again you don't have to. You can still wait until you feel more ready. Don't think that this sets the precedent for you and Griffin."

I nod. "I just don't know what to tell Griffin. I feel like I used him as an escape."

"Be honest with him. Griffin seems like a nice guy. I'm sure he will understand."

"I hope so." I hesitate. "Hey, Aunt Gwen?"

"Yes."

"How come you didn't talk to me this morning? If I told you what happened?"

She lets out a long sigh. "I didn't know where you stood with me. I don't know my place with you right now. I've been thinking about you all day, wondering if you were okay, praying that you would talk to me or someone."

"Does Mom know?" I feel my heart rate increase slightly.

"I didn't tell her." Gwen lies back on her stack of pillows and I can tell that she's getting tired.

"Really? How come?"

"I don't know," she admits. "You told me when you were drunk. It seemed too personal."

"Are you going to tell her?"

"No."

I believe her. She looks different. Her loyalty has always been with my mom but now it seems to have shifted in my favour a bit. "Thanks."

"Anytime." She gives me a small smile. "I miss you." She squeezes my hand.

I try to smile back at her, but I can't. "Should I let you rest now?"

She nods. "I think hearing that you had sex for the first time gave me half a heart attack."

I laugh softly. "Fair enough. Aunt Gwen? Thanks for listening."

"I got you." She closes her eyes. "Don't be a stranger."

"I'll try not to be." I want to hug her, but I don't. I let go of her hand and quietly leave the room. I feel a bit better. I need to talk to Griffin. I'm just walking down the hall when I see Mom walking towards me. She's wearing a long grey coat, a white high neck blouse and a dark pencil skirt. She looks incredible and completely flawless.

"Hi," she looks puzzled as she approaches me. She moves in for a quick hug and I let her embrace me. "What are you doing here?"

"I had my spare last block, so Emma drove me here. I wanted to talk to Gwen."

"Really?" Mom looks half concerned and half like she doesn't believe me.

"Yes, she's asleep now though. Don't worry, I didn't poison her," I say sarcastically.

"Good." She gives me a small smile. "Well if she's sleeping I'll come back later. Most of the snow seems to have melted from this morning. Do you want to go for a quick walk?"

"Sure," I say, hesitantly.

"So how's Gwen?" Mom asks.

"She seemed alright," I tell her as we walk through the entrance doors outside. "She got tired at the end of our visit, but she seemed like her old self."

Mom nods. "What did you guys talk about?"

I have already mentally prepared myself for this question. "Not much. I just wanted to apologize for last night."

"I see." Mom doesn't believe me. I can tell, but she doesn't ask anything more. We walk on a path around the hospital grounds. It's nothing special, a concrete roadway with some shrubs surrounding both sides.

"Mom?"

"Mmhmm." She's looking around and not at me.

"Do you think you could drive me to Griffin's house? I know I'm grounded. I don't need to stay...I just need to talk to him. It will only take a few minutes. Then you can drive me back home?"

She studies my face very carefully. Her eyes and mouth give nothing away and I wonder what she's thinking. "Okay," she says. "Now?"

"Sure."

Mom doesn't say anything the whole way to Griffin's. It's starting to freak me out just a little bit. It's unlike her to be so quiet. She pulls into Griffin's driveway. "I'll be back in five minutes," I tell her, and I get out of the car.

I ring the doorbell and realize that my hands are shaking. Griffin answers. "Hey," he says. He gives me half a smile. "I can't hang out...I'm grounded."

"Me too," I say, pointing to the car. "I just need to talk to you for a minute. Is that okay?"

"Sure." He doesn't move from the doorframe. I notice how nervous he looks. "What's up?"

"I don't know how to say this…"

"You're breaking up with me," he mumbles.

"What? No." I shake my head. "I don't know."

"What?" Griffin bites his cheek on the inside of his mouth, pulling it inward. I hate it when he does this. I think it makes him look like a fish.

"I just wanted to say that I'm sorry about last night. I haven't been able to stop thinking about what happened. I wasn't ready…we shouldn't have…ugh. This is hard. Last night was a mistake. It shouldn't have happened. I was trying to make myself feel better. I shouldn't have done that, and I'm sorry."

"So what are you saying?" Griffin looks confused. "You regret sleeping with me? What's going on with you? I don't get why you're so upset." I still wasn't ready to tell Griffin about Mom and Gwen. I didn't trust him enough. Why didn't I trust him enough?

"Maybe we should just take a step back," I say suddenly. I don't know where it came from.

"What? You just said you weren't breaking up with me." His voice is strained, and he sounds hurt.

"I'm not. I just think we should take a few days to think about things. There's a lot going on right now, a lot that I can't share with you and I just need to go and think about why that is. Okay?"

He stares at me. "Okay," he says quietly.

I kiss him on the cheek. "I have to go. We'll talk soon, okay?" He nods, and I turn and run back to the car. I can feel his eyes watching me as I go.

I get into the car and put my seatbelt on. Mom is talking on her phone. She finishes the conversation and hangs up. "Everything okay?"

I take a deep breath. "I think so."

"Want to go get some dinner?"

"Can we just get takeout and go home? I feel like getting my PJs on and not moving from the couch."

"That sounds like the best thing I've heard all day," she says.

We pick up Chinese food and go home. I don't tell Mom that Griffin and I are taking some time apart. I'm not ready to tell her about what happened. I'm still annoyed at her for everything else. It was easier to tell Gwen because I knew that she wouldn't judge me. Mom judged people for a living. She rarely made mistakes, it seemed she was on a different playing field and that made it harder for me to be open with her sometimes.

After dinner, Mom goes upstairs to shower and I text Gwen and tell her what happened with Griffin. My phone rings and I see her name on it.

"Hello?"

"Texting takes too long," Gwen says.

"Okay." I smile.

"Are you okay?"

"I think so." My admission surprises me. "I wasn't expecting to tell him that. I just realized I couldn't be honest with him about anything going on in my life right now. So I just need to take a few days and regroup, you know?"

"That's very mature of you," Gwen says.

"Thanks." I swing my legs up onto the couch and curl them up into a ball. "How are you feeling?"

"The same," she tells me. "I'm really hoping I only have to be here for a week. I feel like I'm losing my mind."

"I can relate."

"I should get to bed. I'm tired."

"Me too," I say. "Night."

"Sweet dreams," Gwen says and hangs up.

I sit on the couch for a little while longer. Mom doesn't come back downstairs. When I go up her door is closed so I leave it and go to my room. It's not even nine yet but I am exhausted. I curl up under the covers and within seconds fall into a deep sleep.

EIGHTEEN
Kate

My alarm goes off at 5:00am, but I've already been staring at the dark ceiling for an hour. I spent most of the night unable to sleep, tossing and turning in my bed. I've never been much of a worrier; I don't know why my mind has decided to take up this new habit now. I drag my legs out of my bed, not really wanting to go for my run but at the same time knowing that it will clear my head. I put on a pair of thermal running leggings and a thermal pullover. I pull my shoulder-length hair up into a ponytail, secure it with a headband and quietly slip downstairs.

I run for about eight miles, hard and fast and then get to a point where my ankles are starting to ache a little bit too much, so I slow it down to a walk. My mind feels less foggy. I think back to what kept me up most of the night. I don't know why I feel so insecure when it comes to Holly and Gwen right now. Knowing that Holly had visited Gwen and hadn't wanted to talk to me about it was driving me insane. I felt like the two of them were keeping something from me. Honestly, I typically felt like that when it came to Holly and Gwen but now that Holly knew that Gwen was her biological mother, it was slowly pulling me over the edge.

Was it selfish of me to just want Holly all to myself? I didn't want to share my daughter with Gwen. How had Holly just made amends with Gwen so easily? What was going on with her and Griffin? Why didn't she talk to me anymore? I had been racking my brain for hours trying to think of a way to feel more connected to her. To feel less jealous of Gwen. What kind of sister was I? One who was jealous of my sister who was lying in a hospital bed undergoing chemo? Ugh.

I get back home and it's still dark outside. Duane hates that I run in the dark. We've spent countless times in our relationship arguing about the time of day I choose to run – him encouraging me to get a treadmill or a gym membership and me telling him that it would never happen. I'm an outdoor, all-weather runner. Inside the house, I shower and think about the day ahead. Even as an adult I sometimes still get that feeling of wanting to run away and forget everything for a day. I have spent most of my life doing what's expected of me and it can be so draining.

I get out of the shower, wrap a towel around me and call Duane. It's just after six but he gets up early too.

"Hey beautiful," he says into the phone.

"Did I wake you?" I ask.

"Nope," he says. "I've been up most of the night, working on a case."

"I couldn't sleep either. Hey, what's your day like today?"

"The usual."

"Want to play hookie with me?"

"Do my ears deceive me?" Duane laughs. "Kate Sherwood skipping work for a day? Is that even allowed?"

"I do what I want," I say jokingly.

"Where do you want to go?" he asks.

"I don't know," I admit. "I just need to get out of here. I need a break."

"Why don't you drop Holly off and meet me at my house around 8:30?"

"It's a date," I tell him. "I'll see you soon."

I blow dry my hair and curl it into loose curls. I put on some foundation, blush, mascara and lipstick. I don't usually wear a lot of makeup. I prefer the natural look. I put on a pair of dark jeans and a burgundy V-neck sweater. I toss a few things into a travel bag just as Holly walks into my room.

"You're wearing jeans to work?" She gives me an inquisitive look. "Is that even allowed?" It wasn't.

"I'm not going to work," I tell her. "Duane and I are spending the day together."

"Interesting," she smiles mischievously. "Where are you going?"

"No idea," I admit. "I just need a bit of a break."

"I get that." Holly sits down on my bed. I want to ask her what she means, but I'm too fragile right now. My fear of being rejected by my daughter is all encompassing.

"Are you going to see Gwen today?" I ask, feeling my heart race just a little bit more.

"I don't think so," she says. "I might just hang with Emma

afterschool if you won't be around. Is that okay if she comes over? I know I'm grounded."

"That's fine," I tell her. "No Griffin?"

She sighs. "We're taking a break for a few days."

I hesitate before asking. "Everything okay?"

"It will be," she says and doesn't elaborate. I'm hit with a pang of sadness. "Are you okay?" she asks.

"Yeah," I say, quietly. "I'm good. Let's go downstairs, I'll make you breakfast before we leave."

Duane and I drive up into the mountains together. There's a small ski village about 90 minutes from town that we love to frequent. On the way he listens to me vent about Holly and Gwen. Duane is a very patient man.

"I think you should talk to Holly," Duane tells me, tapping his hands on the steering wheel.

"Honestly Duane, I'm so tired of talking. I feel like my entire life for the past three weeks has been a sobbing, blubbering girl-talk fest and I'm over it."

Duane laughs. "Okay, okay. But Katie, you live with two women; it's only fair that your life is like a soap opera sometimes. I think y'all are in a tough spot. Neither of you wants to hurt the other person so you're just tip-toeing around one another. You need to have a boxing round or something. Get everything out on the table."

"That sounds terrible." I half laugh and make a fake afraid face.

"Think about it," he encourages.

"I will." I look out the window and watch the trees blur as we drive down the highway.

It is rejuvenating to spend the day away from Fife Springs. We spend the morning at a hot springs spa. We hang out in the pools, get massages and then Duane takes me for a late lunch.

"This was a good idea," I tell him from across our small, cozy table.

"I'm pretty smart," he winks at me, and his dark eyes sparkle.

"Hey! This was my idea!"

"Oh was it?" He grins. "It was a good idea. I can't remember the last time we spent this much time alone together."

"That makes two of us."

We eat and then go for a walk near a river. It is beginning to warm up and we have some afternoon sunshine, which is a nice break from the morning cold. We walk along a small rocky path together; the water is high but calm. Neither of us talk but it's a comfortable silence. We walk up to a bench and Duane lets go of my hand.

"Let's sit for a minute," he says. He sounds strange, nervous or maybe excited, I can't tell. I raise my eyebrows but do as he says. What happens next is a bit of a blur. Suddenly Duane is on the ground on one knee, pulling a purple box out of his pocket. "Katie," he says. I can see that his hands are shaking. "I've loved you for years. I can't live without you. These past few weeks have made me realize more and more how much we need to quit fooling around and make it official. You're the most beautiful woman I've ever laid eyes on. You're classy, you're funny and you're so smart it's scary. Katie. I'm crazy about you, and I always will be. Katherine Abigail Sherwood, will you marry me?" He opens the ring box. I see the most beautiful ring inside. It's white gold with a halo setting and a large oval diamond in the center.

I don't even have to think this time. "Yes!" I squeal. "Of course I'll marry you." He slips the ring on my finger. I stand up and he embraces me in a tight hug, followed by a long passionate kiss. After all these years, Duane's lips still feel electric on mine. The past few weeks had made me realize how much I needed Duane in my life, how I would feel so empty without him. He was my rock and my steadfast shoulder to cry on. He knew how to make me laugh, how to make me smile and how to make me a better version of myself. I'd spent so many years afraid of being vulnerable and letting myself go. I was now at the point in my life where I was ready to be someone's partner and let myself be taken care of.

After a little while of cuddling and relaxing, we decide to head home. I can't wait to tell Holly and Gwen the news. Duane decides that he wants to cook us dinner so we stop at the grocery store in town. He drops me off at his house to pick up my car and follows me home. As I approach the house I begin to get nervous. I'd barely talked to Holly about my relationship with Duane. I knew she liked him a lot, but with everything that unfolded lately I wasn't sure how she was going to respond to more potentially life changing news.

I park my car into the garage and wait for Duane. "I'm

nervous," I tell him as he approaches me. "I hope she doesn't get mad."

"She won't." He opens the door to the house and I follow him inside. Holly and Emma are sitting at the dinning room table surrounded by books. Studying at the dinner room table usually means business.

"Hi girls!" I give them a small wave with my left hand. I feel like a giddy schoolgirl. "Homework already?"

"Yeah, lit sucks." Holly groans. "We already have two books to read by next week. Like it's the third day of school. Give us a break." Emma nods in agreement. I start playing with my engagement ring; I've been doing this ever since he placed it on my finger hours before; I'm not used to the way it feels.

"Um, what's that on your finger?" Emma asks. Her eyes go wide.

Holly's mouth drops open. "Mom?" She looks at my hand and at Duane. "AHHHHHH!" She shrieks and pounces at my hand. She looks at Duane again. "Are you guys getting married?" I nod. "YES!" She shrieks again and throws her arms around me. I sink in to her hug. It feels so nice to be hugged by her. She grabs my hand again. "It's beautiful! I'm so excited!" She wraps Duane in a big hug too.

"And you were worried she'd be mad," he jokes.

"Mad?" Holly shrieks again. "Never! I'm so happy for you guys. This is the best news!"

"Yes," Emma smiles. She walks over and gives me a hug too. "Congrats!" She high-fives Duane.

"Do you know when you're getting married yet?" Holly asks. She is practically bouncing from toe to toe.

"We were thinking sometime in the fall," I answer.

"Oooo a fall wedding!" Now it's Emma who squeals.

Duane cooks us dinner while Holly and Emma grill me about everything wedding related. I can't help but shake my head that it took a marriage proposal to get my daughter to stay in the same room and speak nicely to me for more than a few minutes. After dinner I know I need to go tell Gwen. Duane goes home and I leave the girls on the couch watching some fitness reality TV show.

Half an hour later I walk into Gwen's hospital room. She doesn't look good. She's paler than I've ever seen her and her skin looks almost green from illness. "Well, well," she croaks out the words as I approach her. "I was wondering when you'd show up." She smiles to show that she's kidding but I'm hit with a pang of guilt.

"Sorry," I say. "I was here yesterday, but you were asleep."

"I was just kidding." Gwen frowns. "You don't need to apologize. I don't expect you to drop your life because I'm in the hospital."

"You don't look so hot," I tell her.

"Thanks a lot."

I laugh. "That was my roundabout way of asking how you're feeling."

"Like shit," she clarifies.

"Don't say shit." I wink at her and she rolls her eyes in response. "Any new news?" I'm concerned that Gwen's chemo isn't going to work.

"I'm getting a blood transfusion in the morning. That's pretty standard though." I hate how she waves off anything medical as standard. She acts like none of it is a big deal. "I'm seriously going to punch you in the nose if you keep waving that massive rock on your finger in front of my face without spilling any details!"

I burst out laughing. "So Duane proposed."

"You don't say!" Gwen's eyes twinkle, despite her murky appearance. "Tell me everything. Do not leave out a single detail!"

I tell her the whole story and at the end she squeals like Holly did.

"Katie, I'm so happy for you." Gwen sits up and gives me a hug. "You deserve to be with someone like Duane. You guys are perfect for each other."

"Thanks," I tell her. I'm beaming.

"Is Holly excited?"

"So excited," I say. "I was so nervous about telling her. She seemed really off yesterday and hasn't really been talking to me with everything that's happened. I didn't know how she would react."

"I'm glad she's happy." Gwen lays all the way back in her bed.

"Has she talked to you anymore?" I ask. I try to say it casually, but fail.

"You mean after yesterday?" Gwen asks. "She just came here to talk to me about Griffin, nothing else. I still don't think I'm her favourite person right now."

"Join the club. At least she talked to you about something," I point out.

"True," she sighs. "It was nice, actually. Talking. It almost felt like it used to, you know, before I drove a wedge through everything."

"All she told me was that they are taking a break?"

"Yeah," Gwen says. "I guess they are. They're young. Kids don't need to be so serious about everything at sixteen."

"Agreed." I know she's not telling me something, but I don't push it.

We sit there for a while, just making small talk and then I leave to let her rest. I kiss her on the forehead before I walk out the door. "Get better so you can get out of here, okay?"

"Working on it." She gives me a weak smile. "Love you."

"You too. I'll call you tomorrow."

I leave the hospital with my mind unsettled. Gwen's happiness for me couldn't hide how sick she was. Honestly, I didn't know what I would do without Gwen in my life. Even when we were apart for all those years it always felt like a piece of me was missing. There was something paranormal about being a twin sometimes. You could feel parts of what the other person was experiencing.

When we were kids and I broke my arm, Gwen who wasn't even with me when it happened, broke out screaming in pain and holding her own arm. Our mom used to call it "Twindrome." I knew Gwen was hurting and it broke me into a million pieces, even when I wasn't with her. As much as it pained me to think about Gwen building a relationship with Holly as something other than her aunt, I needed her to fight like hell to get better. I didn't know if Holly or myself could survive without her, and frankly, I didn't want to find out.

NINETEEN
Holly

The next few weeks are draining. Mom and Duane's engagement seems to be about the only good thing that has happened. Gwen got a cold, which turned into an infection, which put her in isolation. She was in the hospital for an extra week. I didn't go back and see her again, but Mom kept me up to date.

Yesterday, they were finally happy with her bone marrow results and, after three long weeks in the hospital, said her cancer was in remission for now and that she could go home. Remission with leukemia is a bit different; she has to return as an outpatient once a month for consolidation chemotherapy. In her case, this is done as a precaution to eliminate any leukemia cells that weren't killed the first time. Mom has patiently explained this to me several times now. Gwen will take a few weeks off work and slowly start returning, being careful not to overwork herself. Mom and I are doing a bit better. Her engagement seems to be a common interest for us to be able to have a civil conversation with one another.

I still haven't talked to Griffin. We managed to sit on opposite sides of the room in chemistry class, and other than that, I haven't seen him.

I wake up on Wednesday morning feeling like crap. It's the day before Valentine's Day. I have been dreading this day all week. I go downstairs in my pajamas, wondering if I can fake an illness or if I should save it for tomorrow. That would probably be too obvious though. Gwen is sitting at the island drinking a cup of coffee and reading yesterday's paper.

"Good morning," she says.

I nod in response, walk over to the coffee maker, pull a mug out of the cupboard and pour myself a cup of coffee. I've also become hooked on morning coffee. I still hate the taste, but it seems to give me enough of a perk to get me through this brutal semester of school.

"You're chipper this morning," Gwen notes.

"I think I'm sick," I groan. I'm hoping that I can guilt her into letting me stay home before Mom sees me.

"Really?" She gives me a once over. "What kind of sick?"

"Stomach." I take a sip of my coffee and grimace.

"Hmm," she frowns. "Coffee probably isn't the best thing for that. What's up?" I look at Gwen. She looks so much better. Her skin has returned to its golden tan, she had cut her hair short, but surprisingly didn't lose all of it during chemo. She still looks tired, but her green eyes – eyes that match my own – look like they have life in them again.

I study her and I wonder if this is what things would have been like if she had never given me to Mom. Would we have sat in the kitchen together every morning having mother-daughter chats? Would I still have told her about Griffin? Or would she have driven me just as crazy as my own mother sometimes? We still weren't on the best terms. We were speaking and we were friendly but it was still really hard for me to trust her. I hadn't really asked her any of the tough questions yet. I did, however, have no problem running anything and everything boy-related by her.

I sit down beside her. "Tomorrow is Valentine's Day."

"That it is," she closes her paper. "So?"

"So, do you remember Valentine's Day in high school after you and your boyfriend were on a break because you had sex with him and regretted it?"

Mom chooses that moment to walk into the kitchen. "You had sex?" Her eyes go wide.

"Shit," I say, putting my head down on the counter.

"Don't say shit!" Mom and Gwen say at exactly the same time.

"This is too much." I mutter face down from the island. Mom sits down beside me.

"The night of the party?" she asks.

"Yes."

She lightly touches my back. "Were you safe?"

"Yes." This is so awkward I actually want to die. She was not supposed to find out this way.

"Are you okay? Is that why you and Griffin are on a break?"

"I'm okay." I pull my head up. "Yes. I really can't talk about this, Mom."

"Did you know?" she asks Gwen.

Gwen nods. "Yes," she says quietly.

"Big surprise." She looks down at her watch. "Ah. I have to

go." Mom stands up and grabs her briefcase off the floor. She walks over to the coat closet, pulls out her coat and walks out the door into the garage.

"Mom?" I get up and walk after her, but she's already getting into her car. She doesn't respond. I watch as the garage opens and she backs up and drives away. "What just happened?" I ask Gwen who is now standing behind me.

"She's mad that I knew and didn't tell her," Gwen says softly.

"Ah," my mouth forms a frown. "Should I go after her?"

"I'll drive you to school," she says. "Then I'll talk to her."

"You sure? I feel bad," I run my fingers through my hair. "I was going to tell her. I just thought it would be weird. I didn't want her to be mad at me. She's just so perfect, you know? Sometimes I just feel like such a screw-up in comparison. She's probably pissed."

"Hey," Gwen leads me back through the kitchen. "You aren't a screw-up. You made a mistake and, in my opinion, you're dealing with it in a very mature way."

"Maybe you're just saying that because you've been on the inside the whole time," I point out.

"Doubtful," she shakes her head. "Go get dressed."

Fifteen minutes later we are in the car. "Maybe you should just take me to see Mom," I say, pursing my lips and looking out the window.

"I think I should talk to her first," Gwen replies.

"I don't know..." My stomach feels like an empty pit.

"Trust me," she says. "I know Katie, I should talk to her."

"I'm surprised you didn't tell her," I admit.

"I said I wouldn't," she says.

"I know," I clasp my hands together on my lap. "But you always told her everything I told you before."

"That was before," Gwen says.

"Such insight," I narrow my eyes.

"Smart ass," she mutters.

She drops me off at school, and I immediately call Mom. She answers on the second ring.

"Hi," I stammer. "I didn't think you'd pick up the phone."

"What? Why?" She sounds confused.

"Aren't you mad at me?"

"No…"

"But you just walked out and didn't say anything."

"I said I had to go. I did." Her voice is unwavering and hard to read.

"I was going to tell you," I say. I walk over to some steps beside the school and sit down. "I wanted to tell you, I was just scared. I know what you're thinking. I get it. I wasn't telling Aunt Gwen because she's my mom or whatever. My biological mom, you know what I mean. Mom, I was telling her because she's not. I just needed to talk to my cool unbiased aunt – ask her, I even said that." She doesn't say anything. "Mom, sometimes it's hard to tell you things. You're a judge, you judge people for a living. I'm a screw-up, I make a million mistakes and you have it all together. I don't want to let you down." I hear her sigh heavily on the other end of the line.

"A) You're a teenager, you're supposed to make mistakes. B) I don't and won't judge you, ever. C) I don't have it all together, not even close. And D) Holly, sometimes people let people down. That's okay. That's normal. No one's perfect. You're going to let me down. I'm going to let you down. It's how we deal with those situations that help make us better people."

I think about everything she's just said. "So is this speaking in point form a new thing for you or…?"

She laughs. "So much sass."

"Don't be mad at Aunt Gwen, Mom," I say. I hear the bell ring behind me. "She helped me when I was so confused."

"I want to help you," she tells me.

"You do and you have. You're my mom, I don't think you can ever get out of helping me."

"Gwen's your mom too," she whispers. She sounds like she's trying not to cry. I sigh heavily. This is hard.

"Gwen's my biological mom. You're my mom," I have never spoken truer words. There's still so much I want to know from Gwen, but knowing this secret didn't change anything for me in that way.

"Maybe one day you'll think of Gwen as your mom too," she says. "That's okay." I can hear the words cutting through her as she says them. I know it's really not okay, but I also know that she would try harder than ever to make it be.

"I know," I say. "But I don't think that's in our future

anytime soon. Just please don't be mad at her. She just got out of the hospital, she's fragile." I say the last part jokingly (Gwen is anything far from fragile), and Mom chuckles softly on the other end of the line.

"When did you get to be so smart?" She asks.

"I got it from my mama," I say into the phone.

She laughs. "Don't you have to be in class or something?"

"Yes, I'm late!"

"Go. Love you!"

"Love you too, Mom. See you tonight."

I hang up my phone and make my way into the school. I head to my first class and try my best to ignore the pink and red heart decorations that are manifesting throughout the school. I can't help but think that this is going to be a long two days.

TWENTY
Kate

As soon as I hang up with Holly, my phone rings and I see Gwen's name flash across the screen. "Yes?" I answer.

"So cordial," she remarks.

"What do you want?"

"Don't be like this," she says.

"Like what?" I sigh. "Look, I have to get to court so I don't have time –."

"I'm sorry I didn't tell you, okay?" Gwen sounds stressed. "I told Holly I wouldn't."

"That hasn't stopped you before," I point out.

"I guess a part of me liked having something that was just between the two of us," she admits. "I probably should have told you though. But I made sure she was safe, I made sure that he didn't hurt her. She was so mad at me; it was nice that she finally confided in me about something again. I didn't want to break her trust. This just seemed so personal."

Everything she says makes sense. I know if the situation were reversed that I would have felt exactly the same way.

"This is really hard for me," I admit. "Ever since we told Holly the truth, I have just been in a complete panic that she would want you more than me or not look at me the same anymore."

"Katie, Holly thinks the world of you. You're her mom."

"You're her mom too."

"It's different." She sounds sad. "Besides, she doesn't think of me like that. She's also had like four conversations with me in the past three weeks because she's still furious with me. I'm not trying to take Holly away from you. I need you to know that. I will never take her away from you. I hope that one day her and I will have a different relationship, but it will never replace yours. I don't think it ever could."

"I know," I sigh again. "This whole thing is making me act so juvenile. It's preposterous." It was true, my reaction this morning had been child like.

"You and me both," Gwen says. "One step at a time, right?"

"Right," I say. "Sorry, I really have to go. I'm going to be late again tonight. Can you feed Holly for me?"

"I can. Talk to you later."

I hang up the phone and get ready for my morning arraignments. I have over twenty on my docket. It's a long morning in court. By noon, I'm ready for the day to be over. I get an hour break before I need to return. I grab a quick lunch in the courthouse lobby and send Holly a quick text to tell her that Gwen will pick her up from school and that I won't be home until late. So much for a lighter work schedule.

I have another meeting with the Town Council, except this meeting has a portion of it open to the public and they are known to be long and sometimes get a little bit rowdy. I read a text from Duane telling me that I am in no way allowed to work late tomorrow night – apparently he has big Valentine's Day plans for us. Because of the nature of our relationship, Duane and I have actually never had a date on Valentine's Day. He'd snuck a lunch date of course, but never a dinner date because it would have seemed too suspicious. Looking back now, it seems so asinine that we hid our relationship for all those years. I shake my head just thinking about it.

"Hey, beautiful," Duane sits down beside me at the small table I'm at and kisses me lightly on the cheek.

"Hi!" I smile. "What are you doing here?"

"Just had to drop something off when I noticed my drop dead gorgeous fiancé sitting here all alone."

"Well, I was actually just leaving, but this was a nice surprise."

"Did you talk to the ladies?"

"Yes." I had called Duane on my way into the office this morning to vent. "Everything is good now."

"Good, you three are going to need to shape up before I move in."

I laugh in response. I hadn't really thought much about my living arrangements with Duane. I had naturally assumed that he would move in with us, but I wondered what that would look like. Gwen was still staying at the house for the next little bit while she went through chemo, but I wondered how long that would last. Gwen had her own home. I knew part of her reasoning for staying was Holly, but I also knew it likely wasn't permanent.

"Okay, I have to get back. Today is crazy." I lean over and kiss him on the lips. "I love you."

"Love you too, Katie," Duane says. "Call me when you're free."

"Will do." I wave and walk through the courthouse back to my office. I have two more arraignments and then get to do some paperwork. I look out my window and see that it is pouring rain. It looks like we are officially out of snow season and headed into the rainy, dreary part of the end of winter. I hope that spring will make an early appearance this year.

I sit at my desk reading for the next two hours. By five o'clock, my eyes are tired and I feel like I could use a nap. I set my phone alarm, put my head on my desk and take a fifteen-minute power nap. When my alarm goes off, I feel like I could sleep for another twelve hours, so I go out to the lobby and grab a coffee.

With my caffeinated fuel in hand, I make my way outside where the weather is a raging storm. I pull my umbrella out of my bag and open it. I walk as fast as I can to get to my car. The wind is howling, blowing my umbrella upwards and the rain is pounding down sideways, already drenching me. I haven't seen it rain like this in a long time. I get into the car minutes later and am completely soaked. Great. I don't have time to go home and change before my meeting. Not like it would help much anyway, since I still have to walk outside.

I start the car, crank the heat, check my rearview mirror and back up out of my parking stall. I take a right onto Main Street and drive slowly down the main drag of town. My visibility is very restricted, the rain is coming down in sheets and it's hard to see far ahead. Thankfully I don't have very far to go. I pull up to a four-way stop and stop behind the line. There are no other cars waiting, so I go ahead.

I hear a horn blast and turn to look out my window, seeing a massive truck coming towards the side of my SUV. I feel my heart begin to race; I step on the gas. I feel the slam of the impact; the sound of metal crunching, noise is coming from everywhere. That's when everything goes black.

TWENTY-ONE
Holly

School is uneventful as always until the end of the day. I'm waiting for Gwen under the awning out front when I see Griffin walking up to me. I think that the attraction I feel towards Griffin is somewhat supernatural. When I see him I feel like a bubbling idiot and my whole body does this weird sort of tingly/melty thing.

"Hi," I say, my eyes shifting a bit. I wonder what he wants. Good thing it doesn't take long for me to find out. Griffin wraps his right arm around my lower waist and pulls me in close to him. He's taller then me, so his chin almost touches my forehead. "What are you doing?" I ask.

"Shh," he pulls me closer. There is no room between our bodies. He cups the side of my face with his free hands and kisses me. The kiss isn't sweet. It's passionate and full of emotions that are reeling in my mind. He is kissing me like he's never tasted me before and like he doesn't want to stop. I don't want him to stop. Unfortunately time is not on our side as a blasting horn interrupts us.

"Holly," Griffin says, trying to catch his breath. I turn and see Gwen's car. She honks again. I pinch the top of my nose between my index finger and thumb and close my eyes for a second.

"Sorry Griff," I say. "I have to go." I don't give him time to respond as I run the few feet to Gwen's car. I feel the rain pounding down on me and I run a little bit faster. I get in the car and buckle my seat belt. I look over at Gwen. "Hi."

"Hi," she gives me a look. It's a look that says, "What the hell?", but also looks like she wants to high-five me at the same time. "How was your day?"

"Fine." I look ahead as she drives out of the parking lot. "How was yours?"

"Good," Gwen replies. "I went for a walk before this crazy storm started."

"Yeah, this is gross." It's raining so hard you can barely see out the window.

"So I saw you kissing Griffin." I take it back, apparently you could still see out the window. "What's going on?"

"He just came up to me and kissed me," I tell her.

"What do you mean?" Gwen has her eyes on the road.

"That's what I mean. I was just standing there waiting for you and he just came up and kissed me."

"It looked like more than just a kiss," she comments.

"Well it's not like we were having sex on the sidewalk."

"Nice." She rolls her eyes. That must be where I get it from. "Are you guys getting back together?"

"I have no idea. I didn't get to talk to him." I'm not sure why she's prying. Okay, maybe I am, but I'm still annoyed.

"Do you want to get back together?" She bites her bottom lip. I can tell she's hesitant.

"I don't know. Maybe. When he kissed me…I felt it. I forgot what it felt like." I tap my fingers on the armrest.

"I thought the other day you said you wanted to take a break because you didn't know if you could trust him like you should."

"That's true," I tell her. "What's with all the questions?"

"I'm just worried about you," Gwen says.

"Worried? What for?"

"I don't want to overstep," Gwen begins.

As soon as she says that my defenses are up. Gwen never would have said something like that before. She had always been honest and straightforward with me.

"I'm just worried that you're being a little bit reckless. I've wanted to talk to you about this since that night of the party, but I wasn't sure how to bring it up. You need to be careful with the way you choose to express yourself or the way you choose to feel things."

"What does that even mean?" The drive home feels like it's taking extra long because of the weather. I'm ready to peace out of this conversation.

"Drinking and sex, mostly." I can hear the nervousness in her voice. "I just want you to be careful. I don't want you to be like me. I made a lot of bad decisions because I wanted to feel a certain way or just forget something for a night. You can't base logic off of feeling, Holly."

"Okay, I got drunk once and had sex once."

"I know," she says calmly. "It's not about that. It's about why you felt the need to do both of those things."

I get what she's saying, but she's still annoying. She's not my mom. I look over at her. I used to love how I looked like Gwen, but now it's just a painful reminder of a long-kept secret.

"Why don't you just leave the lectures to my mom?" I say coolly. "I already have one parent, I don't need two." I say it to hurt her. The look on her face tells me it worked.

"Okay," she whispers. We drive the rest of the way home in silence. At home I start my homework in my room. I am really having a hard time with organic chemistry. Gwen always used to help me with my math and science homework. I figured it probably wasn't the best time to ask her for help. Knowing Gwen, she would still help me anyway, even though I was being stupid.

Just after six, Gwen calls me down for dinner. She puts some pasta and salad on a plate for me and we sit at the island together. It's strange to me to think that, a month ago, Gwen and I used to do this multiple times a week. I would talk her ears off about my life and she would tell me things about hers. Growing up that would always make me feel extra special that she would trust me enough to confide in me. Now there's just the bitter sting, knowing that she kept such a big secret all of these years.

"This is really good, Aunt Gwen," I say. Despite my anger, it feels weird calling her Aunt now.

"Thanks," she mumbles.

"I'm sorry." I put my fork down. "I don't know how many times I'm going to have to keep apologizing for snapping at you. I understand what you were saying in the car. I get that you don't want me to make the same mistakes you did. I know you're trying to help me. I'm trying really hard to forgive you. It's just not easy. It's so hard. I wish I was better at it."

"It's okay," Gwen says. She turns to look at me. "I get it. Honestly, Holly, you're dealing with this a lot better than I expected you to, and I don't mean that in a bad way."

I'm suddenly not that hungry. "What was it like when you were pregnant with me?" I ask.

"What?" She looks taken back by the question. Her cell phone rings. "It's Duane," she says. "That's strange. Sorry, Holl – let me just see what he needs." I nod. "Hello?" I watch her as she talks. "What do you mean?" She's listening to whatever Duane is saying on the other end. "Is she okay?" I see her eyes get a little bit dim. I notice the frown that appears on her face. "Okay, we are on our way. Let me know if anything changes." She hangs up the phone. "Kate's been in an accident. We need to get to the hospital."

On the way to the hospital I ask Gwen the same questions over and over again. My mom had been driving and had been t-boned by a truck at a four-way stop. She was alive, but unconscious and not in good shape. Gwen is extremely patient with me. When I ask her for the fourth time if she thinks Mom is going to be okay, she takes a deep breath. "Sweetie, I don't know anything else. I'll be able to find out more as soon as we get to the hospital though, okay?"

I nod. Tears fill my eyes. I'm so glad I called Mom back earlier this morning. *Please don't die*, I think to myself.

It takes us longer than usual to get to the hospital because of the storm. I pray that it didn't keep Mom from getting there any faster. When we get to the hospital, I follow Gwen. She heads for the Emergency Intensive Care Unit. The only reason I even know where that was is because I did laps around the hospital the first day Gwen was admitted. I watch as Gwen stands at the front desk and talks to the nurse. I hear nothing. I am completely terrified. All I can think about is my mom. I can't lose her.

I'd never even entertained the idea of anything bad ever happening to Mom. My mother was strong; to me she had seemed invincible. Hell, she never even got a cold! Someone else is standing with Gwen and the nurse now. A doctor. I can't hear what he's saying. I watch them talk to one another. The doctor is talking a lot and Gwen nods. Duane stands beside me.

"Hey Holly," he puts an arm around me. The hug is awkward because he seems tense and distracted. "You okay?"

I don't respond. I keep my eyes on Gwen and the doctor. After a moment, Gwen comes back over to us. She gives Duane a quick hug. "Holly?" I blink. "Come here." Gwen grabs my arm and takes me over to a waiting area; there's only one other person there and some chairs. We stand.

"Your mom is in really rough shape," Gwen says gently. "She isn't responsive, but she's stable. They are running some tests to see how her brain function is, but she's currently unconscious."

"So she might be brain dead?" I say the words so quietly, I'm not even sure if anyone can hear me.

"Let's not think about that right now," Gwen says. "They

need to run the tests before we know anything."

"Can I see her?"

"Soon," Gwen's voice is so calm. I don't know how she's so calm. I want to punch a wall, scream at the top of my lungs or kick something super hard. Why is this happening? Hadn't we been through enough already?

The doctor comes back over and says we can see her now.

"Holly," Gwen says carefully. "She was pretty beat up in the accident, so she might not look like herself. Just be prepared." Be prepared. Right. I take a deep breath and follow Gwen and Duane down the hall. I freeze outside the door. I can't move my legs. "Come on," Gwen says as she takes my hand and brings me inside the room.

I walk in and see Mom lying there. She looks like she is asleep. She is hooked up to a bunch of different machines, which Gwen starts explaining to me, but I hear nothing. Her beautiful dark hair is tousled and a mess. Her face is covered in cuts and scratches. Her left arm is bandaged up. Gwen tells me that her wrist is broken. A tear falls down my face. And then another and another. I feel like I can't breathe again. I want to scream, so instead I turn and run.

I sprint out of the room and down the hall as fast as my legs will move. I run and run through the hospital, to the main entrance and outside on the front patio and finally I stop. I am undercover and see the rain bulleting down on the ground in front of me. I try to breathe but I feel like it's getting harder. Two hands grab my shoulders and turn me around. Gwen is staring at me looking extremely concerned and upset.

"Man kid," she says breathlessly. "You should go out for track."

I lose it. Completely lose it. I start sobbing uncontrollably. Gwen reaches out for me, but I pull away and walk over to the wall.

"Holly," she says gently. She stands beside me. "Come here." She holds out her arms again. I haven't let Gwen touch me since the day she told me the truth. Right now, more than anything I just need someone to comfort me and tell me everything is going to be okay. The stubborn half of me didn't want that person to be Gwen. I look at her; she looks so sad and vulnerable. I take a step towards her. She reaches out and wipes my tear stained cheeks. Then she pulls me towards her and wraps me into a tight hug. I let her.

I cry for a long time. It's not a pretty, dainty type cry either;

it's an ugly, sobbing, heart-wrenching cry. Gwen just holds me the whole time and doesn't say anything. She strokes my hair and squeezes me tight. I think back to all those times that I had wished that Gwen were my mom. I'm overcome with guilt and fear, but at the same time I've never felt so connected to someone in my life. I feel like a part of me that I never knew was missing just became whole again. Realizing this makes me even more of a blubbering mess. Finally, the tears stop. I pull back a bit from Gwen and look at her tear-stained face that I'm only assuming matches my own.

Gwen takes my face in both of her hands. "How can I help you?" she asks, her voice full of concern. I find her choice of words interesting.

"I think I'm ready to talk," I say. I see a bit of panic in her eyes, but she takes a deep breath.

"Okay," she says. "Want to go somewhere inside?"

"Is that okay?"

"Always." She puts her arm around me and we walk back inside together. "Just let me text Duane. He's still with Katie." She does.

Together, we walk down a couple of hallways and then find an empty sitting area. I take a seat on a chair and Gwen sits down beside me.

"At dinner," she said. "You asked me what my pregnancy was like."

"I did," I nod. "I'd never heard any stories of when Mom was pregnant with me or what is was like...now I know why. I was just curious about...I don't know, maybe it's dumb."

"You were curious about where you came from," she smiles. "It's not dumb. It's normal. My pregnancy with you was pretty standard." Gwen typically refers to anyone's medical experience as "standard." "I was really sick at the beginning. I actually didn't know I was pregnant until I was around 10 weeks. I thought I had the flu. It was better in the second and third trimester though. I actually kept a journal during my pregnancy. You can have it if you'd like."

"Really? That'd be cool."

"Holly, my plan was never to give you up. You'll understand this some day when you have a baby of your own. Those first few weeks are so overwhelming. You're a mess from childbirth, all these things are happening to your body that you feel unprepared for and then you're just magically expected to know how to take care of this tiny human that they give you to take home. For me all of those feelings were a trigger. I found myself wanting to go out and get drunk or even smoke again. One night I remember you were screaming and screaming and I couldn't get you to stop and I had to go sit outside for an hour because I couldn't calm you down and I thought I was going to lose it. You still wouldn't stop screaming. I felt unfit to be your mom, Holly. In hindsight a lot of my feelings were probably based on the fact that I didn't have any support. I had no one that could tag me in and out, give me a break, you know? I honestly thought that giving you to Katie was the best thing. Katie was smart, she was calm, and she was perfect on paper and pretty damn close in person. Katie really had her shit together. She still does."

"Don't say shit," I smirk. She laughs.

"I know that it's probably so hard for you to understand this. I thought I was helping you. You were never the problem, the problem was that I couldn't deal with all of the changes in my life."

"I think that makes sense." I sit cross-legged on the chair and stare down at the ugly beige, stained hospital floor. "It still hurts though."

"It hurts me too," Gwen says quietly. "It's hurt me every day since. Not a single day has passed where I haven't wondered what things would have been like if I had kept you. But who knows? Maybe I never would have turned my life around. After I gave you up I saw a doctor and was diagnosed with postpartum depression. I spent years in counselling dealing with my anger and depression from the past, as well as you going away."

"I didn't know that," I say, and then shake my head. "I don't know why I would have known that."

"It's okay," she says.

"Who's my dad?" I ask. This question has been haunting me for most of my life and I'm almost afraid to finally have an answer.

Gwen closes her eyes. She doesn't speak right away. I can tell that she's thinking and that this is hard for her. "His name is Christopher Hawkins. Everyone called him Chris."

"Chris," I say out loud. "Does he know about me?" She shakes her head.

"Chris and I dated in high school. I cheated on him in college and we broke up. That night of the party was the last time I saw him.

He tried calling me, but I never responded."

"So you have no idea where he is…" My heart is racing.

"No," Gwen says, and I don't know if I believe her, but decide to let it go for right now.

I wonder what he looks like. I wonder if she'd ever help me contact him. I think about meeting my dad and try to imagine what that would be like. "So why did you come back?" I am nervous to ask this question, but I've been wondering about it ever since they told me the truth.

"I couldn't handle not knowing you," Gwen said easily. "It really was that simple. I had changed and my life was different. I'd finished school, gone to medical school, was starting my residency. I'd been clean for many years and had finally learned to cope with the past and deal with my emotions in a healthy way. But I wanted my daughter. You were a part of me that I craved every day. I needed to know how you were, what you were like, if you were like me at all…so I came here. Katie and I had been talking on and off for a little while, but she was still furious. I actually thought she was going to slam the door in my face the night I showed up."

"I'm glad she didn't," I cut in. "And I don't think Mom would ever do that."

"True." Gwen gives me a small smile. "She was hesitant to let me see you though, with good reason. After a few days and a lot of talking, she introduced us. You were the most beautiful little girl I had ever seen. You had gorgeous blonde curls and green eyes just like mine. Our resemblance was eerie if you didn't know our background. I guess this was something Kate had always been concerned about, but no one ever questioned it. You were Katie's girl, you just looked a lot like her twin sister."

"Can I tell you a secret?" My heart beats a little faster. Gwen nods. "I used to wish that you were my mom. I've never told anyone that before. When Mom was working all the time and you were always around. You were just always so fun and we've always had such a great connection…until recently." I feel my lips fall into a sad frown.

"I used to wish that too." Gwen takes my hand. "Sweetie, I need you to know this hasn't been easy for me. There were some days where it pained me to be so near to you and have you not know the truth. But I kept telling myself that it was better for all of us if I could just be your favourite Aunt Gwen."

"I understand why you did it." I clasp my hands together and squeeze them hard. "I kind of wish you'd told me all of that stuff from the beginning. It probably would have made it easier to understand. I still think it's going to take some time from my end, but I don't hate you."

She smiles. "Well, I can live with that."

"So what happens now?" My heart is feeling a bit lighter, but my head is pounding and my brain is filled with worry over Mom.

"With what?"

"With us? What do we do now? Things aren't just going to be the same as they always were…"

Gwen frowns. "I know. I think we just need to take things slowly. I'm not going to try to be your mom and I know you don't need another parent."

"I didn't mean that." I look her in the eyes. "I'm an idiot. Aunt Gwen, you've always been like another mom to me, you know that. I just don't know what you are now."

"How about somewhere in between?" She suggests. "We can figure it out together as it happens."

"Okay," I say. My mind can't help but wander back to Mom. "Do you think she's going to pull through?" My lips are quivering and I notice my hands shaking. I don't even realize that I'm crying until Gwen wipes some tears off of my cheeks. "I've been terrible to her, Gwen. I've been mean and distant and I wouldn't even let her touch me. I just felt so betrayed by her. I wanted her to hurt like I was and now I just hate myself for it."

"Oh babe." Gwen gives me the saddest smile. She grabs my arms and pulls me over to her. Then she does something that would look beyond strange to anyone watching us. She lifts me up into her lap. Like I'm three years old. She holds me on her lap like a baby and cuddles me close to her. "Your mom knows how much you love her, Holly. She's crazy about you. She wouldn't want you to feel this way. She loves you more than anything in the world." She holds for a little while longer and comforts me as I cry.

"How about we go see how Katie is doing?" she asks me. "I'll stay with you. We can try to make it a little less scary."

"Okay," I say nervously. I slide off her lap and she stands up. We start walking back to the ICU together. "How are you so calm?" I ask.

"I'm a doctor," she reminds me. "I stay calm for a living. My mind is trained to see things differently than you do. From the outside, people will look at a patient and see everything that is wrong. This brings forth panic. When I see a patient, my mind immediately begins to assess the situation. How can I fix this? What steps to I need to take to prevent the worst outcome and to improve the current situation? I don't just look at the end result, I look at the steps that need to be taken to change it."

"Hmm," I mumble, taking in everything that she's just told me. "Makes sense I guess. That sounds like it would hurt my brain though." She winks at me and takes my hand. We're outside of Mom's room now. "I don't know if I can see her like this again," I say. I feel like a coward.

"Sure you can," Gwen says easily. She leads me into the hospital room. Duane is sitting beside the bed with his head down. He looks up at us as we walk in. "Hey," Gwen says softly. "You can take a break for a bit. Go get some coffee or something."

Duane nods. He stands up, walks past us and gives me a pat on the shoulder.

"Come over here," Gwen says to me. I follow her to the side of the bed. "We are afraid of what we can't see. These machines look scary, but right now they are helping your mom fight like hell. This here is keeping her hydrated, it's for fluids. See how they go through here into the IV? This next machine is monitoring her heart. It will also detect anything irregular that might happen. That can be normal if your body is in shock."

I watch Mom. She looks surprisingly peaceful, despite her banged up face and shoulder. She almost has a small, smile on her face. She is still so beautiful.

"You can touch her if you want," I hear Gwen say.

I take both of Mom's hands. I look at her red, battered knuckles and run my fingers over them. I bend over and whisper in her ear. "I love you, Mommy." I am shaking all over. "I'm here waiting for you. And I'm sorry for everything." I kiss her on the forehead. Gwen rubs my back. I sit next to her, holding her hand for what seems like an eternity.

Eventually Duane comes back into the room. He and Gwen stand over by the door talking for a few minutes.

"Holly?" Gwen calls. I look over at her. "We should figure out a game plan for tonight. Duane or I can take you home or –."

"I'm staying here," I say immediately.

"You might feel better if you get some rest at home," Gwen tells me.

"Let her stay," Duane says. "She wants to be near her mom. We can all stay." So we do. Duane sleeps in the chair beside Mom's bed and Gwen and I share the small, old leather window loveseat.

I feel like I barely sleep. Every hour a nurse is in to check Mom's vitals. She remains stable throughout the night – at least I think she does based on the conversations I hear. I open my eyes and wonder what time it is.

"Good morning," Gwen says beside me. We are sandwiched together on the couch, our faces only a few inches apart.

"Hey," I say back.

"Did you sleep much?"

"Nope. You?"

"Nope." She pulls herself up into a sitting position and I turn my body to do the same. I watch as Gwen braces herself to stand up. I notice that she wobbles a bit.

"Are you okay?" I speak with concern.

"I'm fine," she reassures me. "I'm just going to talk to the doctor and then we can go get some breakfast, okay?" I nod in agreement. Duane is still asleep in the chair beside Mom's hospital bed.

When Gwen is gone I quietly cross the room and enter the bathroom. I empty my full bladder and then stand in front of the mirror examining myself. I am the physical definition of a hot mess. My eyes are bloodshot; my skin is pale with blotchy streaks from yesterday's tears. My blonde curls hang around my face in an untamable mane. I look like a train wreck. I turn on the tap and splash some ice cold water on my face. I wet my hair a bit and pull it up into a messy ponytail.

I leave the bathroom and Gwen is already outside waiting. "You good?" she asks. I nod and together we leave the room.

I walk beside Gwen as she leads me to the cafeteria. Gwen is quiet while we walk and I know that this means she is thinking. Gwen doesn't like to talk when she's processing her thoughts.

The hospital cafeteria is nothing special. There are tables and chairs scattered around, a coffee bar and a big food line. It smells like coffee and eggs.

I walk through the food line and veto the breakfast meat and camp eggs – the eggs that are so compacted you can get them out with an ice cream scoop. I decide on a bagel and some coffee. Gwen takes the same. She pays for our food and we sit at a small two-person table by a large row of windows.

"So what did the doctor say?" I ask Gwen. I open my bagel and spread some cream cheese from a tiny pack on one side of it.

Gwen takes a sip of her coffee. She winces when she realizes how hot it is. "Not much," she shrugs. "She's stable, but no change. That's not a bad thing. It's just a waiting game right now. They might be able to tell us more during rounds in a couple of hours." Gwen takes a deep breath and closes her eyes.

"Are you feeling okay?" I ask.

"I'm just a bit nauseous," she admits. "And tired. All this stress isn't the greatest for my body."

"I thought you didn't get stressed," I roll my eyes. This was a common claim of Gwen's.

"Everyone gets stressed," she speaks slowly. I'm not used to this open, vulnerable Gwen. I'm more familiar with her joking and teasing. It's a weird adjustment.

"I know." I take a bite of my bagel. I don't feel hungry, but I know I need to eat.

"How about I take you home after this?" Gwen says. "You can get cleaned up, grab whatever you need and we can be back here before rounds. I have a follow-up appointment with Dr. Anderson this afternoon and I need to get some blood work done too."

"Sure," I tell her. "So you're not going to try and make me go to school?"

"I'm not special," she laughs. "You can stay here for while. We can go back and forth. Get Emma to bring you your homework though, okay? You still need to do the work."

"I will."

"Good." She pushes her coffee away. "I wonder when I'm going to be able to stomach regular food again."

"How long do chemo side effects last?" I put my bagel down. I don't feel hungry.

"A while." Gwen sighs and stands up. "Let's get out of here."

We get home in record time where we both immediately head for the shower. After a quick shower, I dab some product in my hair and change into some new clothes. I put another change of clothes, my phone charger and my schoolbooks into a large shoulder carry-on bag. Gwen is waiting for me in the kitchen. Her shower has given her skin back some colour and she's munching on an apple.

"You ready?"

"Yup."

I spend the first half of the car ride to the hospital worrying about Mom and praying that she will wake up. Thinking of the alternative is too much for my brain, so I pick a new subject to torture myself with instead.

"What was he like?" I say the words to Gwen very slowly, very carefully. I watch her face change. I see it go from confusion to panic to worry in about ten seconds.

"Chris?" she clarifies.

"Yeah, my dad." I see her cringe at my words, and I turn away from her to look out the window.

"This is hard for me to talk about," she admits.

I don't respond. The car is silent for a minute or two before she answers me.

"Chris was my first love. He was smart and kind. He was handsome and a bit of a nerd. He was extremely uncoordinated. He was funny. He could make me laugh for hours." Gwen's voice is soft and nostalgic.

"Sounds like a keeper," I turn my body to face her.

"He was," she sounds sad again. She parks the car in the hospital parking lot. We get out, grab our things and start walking towards the entrance.

"Do I look like him? I mean, I know I look like you, but –."

"You have his smile," she interrupts me. "The way your face changes when you smile. You look just like him."

I smile when she says this. She looks like she's going to say more, but she doesn't. I wonder where he is and what he does. Maybe he has a family of his own. Would he even want anything to do with me if I found him? We continue walking towards Mom's room.

"What are you thinking about?" Gwen asks. I can hear the way she's asking and her voice sounds like she doesn't want me to give her an answer.

"I'm just curious about him," I admit. "I wonder if he'd like me." Gwen stops walking and looks directly at me.

"He would love everything about you," she tells me. "I know

you're curious about Chris and I get it," she pauses. "But I think we should wait until your mom wakes up and talk to her first. Can you do that for me?"

"Yes," I nod. Suddenly my eyes fill with tears thinking about Mom. My bottom lip starts to quiver. Gwen puts her hands on my shoulders as if to steady me.

"It's going to be okay, kiddo. Let's go see how she's doing, alright?"

I nod and follow her the rest of the way to the room. We get to the room and Duane is still beside the bed, holding a cup of coffee.

"Hey," he nods at us as we enter the room. His eyes are red and glazed over. "The doctor will be back in a few minutes." I sit on the arm of Duane's chair and put my hand on Mom's arm. Duane loosely wraps his arm around me.

"How are you holding up, Holl?" he asks me. His brown eyes are filled with concern and empathy.

"I've been better," I shrug. "You?"

"Same," he gives me a weak smile. "Hopefully we'll get some answers today."

On cue, Mom's doctor walks into the room. He greets us all and I listen as he tells Duane and Gwen about the next steps for Mom. He tells them that all of her vitals are stable and now they are just waiting for her to wake up. It should be any time now.

I'm immediately filled with anxiety that this is not going to go well. I kiss Mom on the cheek, pick my bag up off of the floor and walk past Gwen and Duane out of the room. I need a distraction while I wait. I round the corner and see a waiting area filled with a few chairs, tables and couches.

I sit down at a table and pull out my chemistry textbook. Emma had emailed me all of my homework the night before. I open the book to the week's chapter review and spend a few minutes staring at it before realizing I have no clue what I'm doing. I dive into the world of moles and matter and for a while I'm so absorbed in my work that I don't even notice Gwen walk into the waiting area.

"How's it going?" Her voice is gentle as she sits down beside me. I shrug in response.

"Just working on some chemistry."

"Need any help?"

"No," I mutter. "Yes," I say right after.

Gwen peers over at my textbook. "The wonderful world of moles. I can help you."

"Okay." I sigh and lean back in my chair.

"No change yet," Gwen says. "She's doing really well though. She must be having a really good sleep." She's trying to lighten the mood, but it doesn't work for me. I close my eyes and take a deep breath.

"I know it's rough." She clasps her hands together. "I think she'll pull through though. Katie is strong."

I nod. She was right. My mother was the strongest person I knew, hands down. She had raised me alone while in law school, become a lawyer, as well as one of the first female judges in our town. She was literally the definition of a pillar.

"Do you think it's okay if I get out of here for a bit later?" I ask Gwen. "I just need some air. I was thinking of going to Emma's after school."

"I think that's a good idea. It will be good to have a change of scenery."

We hadn't even been at the hospital for 24 hours and I felt like I was going insane. The machines, the people, the smell – it was all too much for me to take in.

"I can give you a ride if you need one," Gwen offers.

"I'll talk to Emma and let you know."

Gwen nods. "I have to go meet with Dr. Anderson in a bit, but I can help you now if you want?"

"Sure," I say. I point to question seven. "I don't know how to convert this."

"Let me see." She grabs the book and starts reading through the page. "Hmm, mole conversion. I hate organic chem."

"What?" I fake a shocked look on my face. "You mean you don't remember everything you learned from your science degree? Organic chem doesn't apply to your every day scenarios at the doctor's office?"

Gwen laughs. "Not even a little bit."

"Fantastic. Can you tell my teacher that?"

"We all need to learn it, girl. Okay, watch me." She quickly works out the equation on the page and then explains it to me. Then she gets me to do it for her. Gwen is a math wiz. She has been my own personal tutor growing up.

"Thank you, thank you, thank you!" I say, after working

through a few of the problems on my own. "Remind me again why I took chemistry?"

"Probably because your mom wants you to be well rounded," she remarks

"It's true," I sigh.

"Okay." Gwen looks at the clock on the wall. "I need to head for a bit. Are you good?"

I nod. "I'll go see how Mom is and then do some more homework."

"I'll come find you later." Gwen stands up and waves as she exits the room.

I go to check on Mom. She is still the same. I sit next to her, hold her hand, and begin to pray. I want to talk to her more than anything right now. There's an ache in me that is longing to sit with her, to share, to be held. I want to talk to her about Gwen and about my dad. I want to smack myself for being so rude to her for the past few months. If I had known this would have happened I would have been different. I promise myself that when she woke up – if she woke up – that things would be different between us.

After staying with her for an hour, I go back to the sitting area and do some reading for English lit. It's the early afternoon when Gwen finds me and hands me a sandwich.

"How was your appointment?" I ask after taking my first bite. It tastes like cardboard, but I'm suddenly so hungry that it doesn't matter.

"Good." Her lips form a tight smile. "Chemo is doing its job."

"I'm glad."

"Me too." She pauses. "It will just take a bit to feel normal again I guess. I'm cleared to go back to work next week."

"Are you going to?" I ask, my mouth full. I take a sip of water.

"We will see how things go," she replies. Gwen takes a sip of her drink. She looks distracted.

"Can you drive me to Emma's now? She has a spare last block, so she's already home. Her mom said I'm good to come for dinner."

"I can. I have to meet Andrew in a little bit, so I can drop you on my way and pick you up later. Does that work?"

"Yup," I tell her. I start packing up my things.

Half an hour later I walk into Emma's house. It's already a circus. Her brother Jeremy who is a year older than us is in the living room hanging out with a few of his friends. We walk into the kitchen where her younger twin sisters are studying at the table. Below them in the split-level den, I can see her youngest brother Justin playing video games with one of his friends. Emma's house is always packed with people. I love it. It's a refreshing change from my very quiet house.

Emma's mom, Adele, walks into the kitchen. "Holly, sweetheart! How are you? How's your mom? She's been in our prayers." She takes me into her arms, embracing me for a moment. She then holds me back and examines me. "Are you okay? You look tired. Have you eaten?" I can't help it, I laugh. It feels nice to be fussed over.

"Mooooom, please!" Emma shakes her head. "Give the girl some breathing room."

Adele smiles. "Have a cookie." She holds one out to me and I take it from her. The cookie is amazing. I devour it in about ten seconds.

"Mom's okay," I answer after. "Her vitals are normal and she seems strong. They are just waiting for her to wake up…any time now."

"That's great news." Adele is the complete opposite of my mom. My mom is put together and careful; Adele is eccentric and busy. Her dark hair is always a wild mess, her clothes are typically mismatched and she is often running frazzled from one place to another. With five kids, her life is chaotic, but the only thing I've always noticed about Adele Fields is that she always has a smile on her face –not a forced smile, but a genuine one. Her laughter carries throughout her house and it makes me happy. "And how's Gwen doing?"

"She's good. Tired, but that's normal. She had an appointment today and everything was looking good."

"I'm so glad." Adele lets out a long sigh. "Your poor family. You guys have been through so much lately." I know Emma has told her mom about everything that has happened between Mom, Gwen and I.

"It's been pretty crazy." I put my hand on the kitchen counter as if to balance myself.

"If you ever need anything at all, Kevin and I are here for you," she smiles at me. Kevin, Emma's dad, is the high school principal, which is always fun for her and her siblings.

I smile back at her. "Thank you so much."

Emma grabs my arm. "Let's go somewhere quieter," she says.

"Good luck!" Adele calls after us. I can hear her laughing as we walk out of the room.

"Upstairs," Emma says in a sing-song voice as she pulls me towards the stairs behind her. We go up to Emma's room. Emma has her own room, which is nice for her. She used to share with her sisters when they were younger but a few years ago her parents turned their attic into a loft for Jeremy, and Emma got his room.

"So are you going to find your dad?" Emma asks the second we sit down on her double bed.

I roll my eyes at her. "Way to bury the lead."

"Well it's kind of a big deal."

"I know," I sigh. "I want to talk to my mom about it first. I want to see what she thinks. He doesn't even know that I exist."

"I wonder what he's like," she says thoughtfully.

"Gwen made him sound picture perfect."

"That's surprising coming from Gwen."

Emma wasn't wrong. Gwen was even pickier than Mom when it came to men. I don't think she had dated anyone for more than a few weeks the whole time I'd known her. She was knit picky and seemed to want something that didn't exist.

"What's new with you?" I change the subject.

"Not much," she shrugs. "Carter asked me out." She references a boy from our friend group who I haven't talked to in weeks.

"Shut up! Really?"

"Yup."

"Did you say yes?"

"Maybe," she grins. "We are going out this weekend."

"That's so great. It's about time."

"That's what he said too."

I lay back on her throw pillows and we are quiet for a few minutes. It's a nice, familiar quiet. I feel safe with Emma.

"Have you talked to Griffin?" She wraps her arms around a pillow and hugs it to her chest.

"No." I make a face. "He texted me to say sorry about Mom and that was it. I need to talk to him though. I just need everything to slow down a little first."

Emma nods in agreement. "That sounds reasonable." Her mom calls us for dinner and we head downstairs to the dinning room.

Dinner with Emma's family is like Thanksgiving every night. A table full of people with great food and conversation. During the middle of dinner my phone rings. I see Gwen's name and mouth a "sorry" to Emma's parents as I leave the table to answer it.

"Hello?" I say into the phone.

"Holly," Gwen's voice is excited, a bit breathless. "Your mom is awake! I'm on my way, I'll be there in five minutes."

My eyes fill with tears, a smile forms on my face, and excitement and anxiety run through me all at once. "Really? She's okay?"

"She's doing really well," Gwen says. "She wants to see you."

"Good," I smile. "I'll wait outside. See you soon."

I am practically bouncing on my seat the whole way to the hospital, asking Gwen a million questions the whole way there. How is she? What does she remember? Have they noticed any permanent damage or anything else?

Gwen informs me that besides her broken arm, she is doing really well. So far her vitals are still stable and she seems to be functioning normally. She tells me they will likely monitor for a couple of days and then she can go home.

When we get to the hospital I am suddenly so nervous that I am beside myself. I follow Gwen to Mom's room, I can't wait to see her for myself and know that she's okay. I can't wait to start over and get it right this time.

TWENTY-TWO
Kate

I'm not usually an impatient person, but then again I'm not usually a person who ever has to wait for much of anything. Waiting to see Holly was agonizing. I hadn't even been awake for an hour, and I was already growing agitated. Duane sat beside me; he had been next to me when I woke up, slightly confused and disoriented. Duane was being amazing – feeding me juice and making sure I was okay. A nurse had been checking my vitals every fifteen minutes religiously and I was already over this place.

"Can you tell her I'm fine?" I pout to Duane when the nurse leaves the room.

"You were just in a coma for over twenty-four hours," he points out.

"I know. I just want to see Holly."

"She should be here any minute," he smiles. "I'm so glad you're okay.

"I know, I got that the first ten times you told me," I wink at him.

"So it was a bit of overkill."

"You're sweet. I love you."

"I love you too." He leans forward and plants a kiss on my chapped lips. I wonder if Gwen has any Chapstick.

The door to the room opens and Gwen walks in with Holly trailing behind her. "I'm going to go home and get cleaned up," Duane tells me. "I'll call you later?"

"Sounds good. Thanks." I fix my eyes on my daughter standing in front of me. She looks tired. There are dark circles underneath her green eyes. I notice her eyes look sad, but a look of relief floods her face the moment her eyes meet mine. "Hi baby," I motion her over towards me.

"Mommy," she says in a childlike voice. She runs over to the bed and lunges herself into my arms. "I'm so glad you're okay," she whispers to me. I put my lips to her head. I'm so focused on Holly that I don't even notice Gwen slip out of the room.

"Me too," I tell her.

"I'm so sorry, Mom. I feel like everything has been such a mess lately. I've been such a jerk to you. It's been making me sick this whole time. When I thought I could maybe lose you I was beside myself." She starts to cry.

I pull her closer to me so that she is now sitting on the bed beside me. "It's okay. I'm okay. We're okay." I continue to hold her in my arms as she cries for a few more minutes.

When she stops crying she sits up straighter but still stays cuddled up to me. I'm not used to this version of Holly. I'm more familiar with the girl who dodges a hug from me and doesn't like to get too close.

"Does your arm hurt?" She asks me.

"Not as much as my head did when I woke up," I laugh. "They gave me some pain killers. They will cast my arm tomorrow and hopefully if my vitals stay the same I'll be able to go home in a couple of days."

"That's what Gwen said."

"How are things with you and Gwen?" I ask, my voice showing genuine concern. Holly has been through so much in these past few weeks, I don't know how she's holding it all together.

"Better," she admits. She looks a bit uncomfortable.

"You can talk to me about it," I offer.

"I know, it's just a bit weird, not talking to you – just everything with Gwen." I nod and she continues. "Gwen told me about my dad. His name is Chris Hawkins. She told me that he doesn't know about me and that she hasn't seen him since."

I raise my eyebrows and try not to let my face give anything else away. Chris was Gwen's highschool boyfriend. He had followed her to college and they had tried to make it work. I wasn't surprised that he was Holly's father, I had always wondered. It was the later that had surprised me. Gwen had to know where Chris was and, if she didn't, she could easily find out. His parents still lived in the town where we grew up. I didn't want to lie to Holly, but I also wanted to talk to Gwen and give her a chance to be honest again. I wasn't sure what her reason was for not being open about this. My guess was that she was afraid of what would happen if Holly wanted to find Chris.

"How are you doing with all of this?" I ask Holly, rubbing her shoulder. She pulls into me even closer.

"It's hard. Honestly Mom, the only thing I've cared about these past twenty-four hours is that I would get to see you again."

"You can't get rid of me that easily," I joke.

"I was terrified," she admits.

"I know," I feel my own eyes fill with tears. I can't imagine ever losing Holly. It was one of the reasons that I had kept Gwen's secret for all these years.

"Did you know my dad?" She asks.

"I did," I reply. "I haven't seen him in a long time though. We all grew up together. I didn't go back home for our ten-year reunion, so I think the last time I saw him was at my parents' funeral."

"Did Gwen go to your ten-year reunion?"

"I'm honestly not sure, sweetie. That was the year before we started talking again. She never mentioned it to me if she did." That wasn't a lie. I had no idea what Gwen had been up to. I hadn't heard Chris' name since they broke up in college.

Holly turns and looks me in the eyes. Her green eyes look determined and I brace myself for her next question. "Mom…I was wondering…" She stops talking and looks uncertain.

"If you want to find him I'll help you," I offer softly, ignoring the jabbing pain of twin guilt forming in my stomach. "If that's what you were wondering."

"Really?" Her eyes light up a little and I see a small glimmer of hope in them.

"Of course," I nod. "Every girl should get to know her father. We should talk to Gwen about this too, but if you want to meet him I will help you in anyway that I can."

It doesn't bother me to think about Holly meeting her dad, especially now that I know who he is. What bothers me is that Gwen might still be keeping secrets from the both of us. I push my thoughts aside and tell myself that I can deal with Gwen later.

"I know it was only twenty-four hours, but I missed you so much," Holly says, playing with the blanket on the bed.

"I missed you too," I pat her gently on the leg. "And it sounds like you had a pretty crazy twenty four hours."

"I want things to be different," Holly says with determination. "I want things to be like they used to be between us. I know that so much has changed, but I just need my mom. I didn't realize how badly until you weren't there."

My heart aches for Holly, who I know is falling apart looking for answers and some type of resolution to everything that has been handed to her. "I'd like things to be different too," I say. She smiles at me and begins to share more. We talked about school and she tells me about Griffin and how confused she is. She tells me about the rest of her conversation with Gwen and how she's not sure what to make of their relationship right now. An hour later my heart is full and I feel like I finally have my daughter back.

Gwen eventually reappears in my room and asks what our plan is. I tell her that she and Holly should go home for the night. That way they can get a good night's sleep and come back in the morning. Holly doesn't want to leave, but after a bit of convincing she reluctantly allows Gwen to take her home.

I'm exhausted when they leave. The nurse comes back and gives me some more pain medicine. I feel like I could fall asleep, but I call Duane to say good night.

He answers on the second ring. "Hey babe. I was just about to leave the station to come and see you. I had to stop in and take care of a few things."

"I just called to tell you not to come." I smile, knowing that he had planned on coming back.

"Why not?"

"I'm exhausted. Holly and Gwen just left. Come see me tomorrow though?"

"I'll be there first thing. You can fill me in then. I love you."

"Love you too. Good night."

"Night princess." He hangs up.

I put my phone down on the stand beside my bed. I adjust the bed back a bit with my right arm – my good arm – and sink back on the too-flat hospital pillow. I close my eyes and drift off to sleep.

I wake up early the next morning. Well, I've been woken up hourly for most of the night. They take out my catheter and I'm now able to get up and use the washroom and take a shower. When I step out of the shower I feel like a new person. I hug my blue hospital gown to me and take a look in the mirror. My face looks like I've been in a punching match with someone. My left eye is swollen and black, there are several red surface scratches on my face and what's not marked up is a pale, clammy white.

Back in my hospital room I text Gwen and ask her to bring

me some clothes and makeup. I feel antsy so I walk around the room for a few minutes and stretch out my arms and legs. It feels strange for me to not run first thing in the morning; it's like my body is craving it, even in its tired, worn-out state.

Duane shows up half an hour later. He hands me a coffee and a paper bag with a bagel in it. "Bless you," I say to him after taking my first bite. "You don't want to know what they tried to feed me for breakfast here."

"Hospital food isn't your favourite?" He winks at me.

"Not even my second favourite." The bagel is heavenly. A fresh blueberry bagel with strawberry cream cheese, my favourite breakfast splurge. I love that Duane knows this. I study him for a moment. He looks tired. He has dark bags under his eyes and his normally clean-shaven face is full of stubble.

"What?" Duane asks, noticing me watching him.

"Nothing," I shrug. "Just admiring this new caveman look you have going for you."

Duane runs his fingers through his dark hair and frowns at me. "It's been a crazy few days."

"I'm just teasing."

"I thought I was going to lose you." He sighs a heavy sigh and takes my hand in his.

"You couldn't get rid of me if you tried," I wink at him.

"When you get out of here, let's set a date," he insists. "I don't think I can wait much longer to marry you."

I smile. "I think that sounds like the best thing I've heard all day."

Duane doesn't stay for long. When he leaves they take me to put on my cast. I choose white. It's a short cast that ends just below my left elbow. I have to wear it for six weeks. When I get back to my room, Gwen and Holly are there.

"Nice armor," Gwen comments, acknowledging my cast.

"I'm surprised you didn't get black," Holly says.

"They didn't have it," I tell them. "I asked." They both laugh.

We chat for a while and then I look at the clock on the wall. "Gwen, you should get Holly to school," I say.

"I want to stay with you," Holly interjects immediately.

"I know," I smile at her. "You missed school yesterday though, so you should go. I don't want you to get behind."

"It's Friday," Holly says, like this should have some kind of impact on my decision. "And Aunt Gwen was helping me with my chem."

"I think I'm probably going to get to go home today," I explain. "So if you go to school, by the time you're done, I'll hopefully be on my way home. Then we have the whole weekend to spend together."

"Fine," Holly pouts. "I'll text Emma. She can pick me up on her way."

I nod. "Sounds good." I want to talk to Gwen. I haven't had a minute alone with her since I've been awake. Holly must sense this. She tells us that Emma is on her way and that she's going to wait out front. She gives me a hug and leaves. I notice she doesn't hug Gwen and I wonder why. Gwen is standing at the end of my bed looking out of place. This is an unusual way for Gwen to appear.

"Come sit," I say to her. She sighs softly and walks over to the chair beside my bed and sits down. "I feel like I missed a lot while I was out."

"You did," Gwen acknowledges.

"How are you?" I ask her.

"Holly told you about Chris," she says.

"Yes," I confirm. "But how are you?"

"I'm okay," she shrugs. Sometimes getting information out of Gwen is like pulling teeth – stubborn and annoying.

"Are you feeling okay? How was your follow up appointment?"

"Just tired. And it was good. My blood work was good, I need another treatment in two weeks."

"I'm happy to hear that."

"I know, me too. I'm supposed to go back to work on Monday."

"That will be good for you."

"I think so," Gwen nods.

"Things seem better between you and Holly."

"I think they are," she says. "It's still unfamiliar territory...I think it will just take time to figure out."

"For sure." We are quiet for a minute. "So Chris Hawkins, hey?" Gwen nods in response. "I guess I shouldn't be surprised."

"Did Holly ask you about him?"

"She did," I look away from Gwen and start tracing outlines on my cast. "She said you didn't know where he was."

"Well, that's not entirely true," Gwen's voice is shaky and filled with guilt.

"I figured."

"He still lives at home."

"Like with his parents?"

"No," she laughs. "In Alder." Alder was the town we had grown up in. It was similar to Fife Springs in size, but an hour and a half away. "He's a teacher there."

"How do you know that?"

"Julie told me." Julie was a girl we had gone to high school with. She and Gwen had an annual girls weekend every year.

My eyes go wide. "Does Julie know?"

"No. God no. I told you Katie, I've never told anyone this."

"Why didn't you just tell Holly the truth?" I sigh, knowing that history was going to repeat, and I was going to have a crushed teenage girl on my hands.

"I panicked." A pained look forms on Gwen's face. "I wondered what she would think and if she would want to meet him."

"She already wants to meet him, Gwen. He's her father."

"I know, I know." She holds up her hands in retreat. "I'm just being stupid. I wasn't ready for all of this."

I grab her hand with my good one. "Let's just take it one step at a time, okay?"

They decide that I can go home that afternoon. I have to come back next week for a checkup. No driving until then, and I am ordered to take the next week off work to rest. I'm not particularly thrilled about this, but I know better than to argue with a doctor.

After lunch, I'm discharged from the hospital and Gwen drives me back to the house. "Hey," I ask her suddenly. "What happened to my car?"

"Duane took care of all that," she tells me. "He has a rental for you on Monday until your replacement comes in."

"Nice." I stare out the window as she pulls into the driveway and breathe a sigh of relief as I see my house in front of me. It feels good to be home. I get out of Gwen's car and slowly walk up the path towards the house. I brace myself, as I still feel a bit wobbly walking. Gwen helps me inside and helps me get settled in the living room on the couch.

"Do you need anything?" she asks me.

"Doesn't this whole situation just scream irony to you?" I snuggle back into the couch cushions and rest my casted arm on the end of the couch.

"What do you mean?" Gwen squints her eyes at me.

"You have cancer," I point out. "I should be taking care of you."

Gwen shrugs. "I'm in remission?"

I smile at her. "Still. Thanks for taking care of me. And for taking care of Holly, too. I really appreciate it, Gwen. I know we have our moments, but I really do appreciate all you do for us."

"I know." She looks sad. "You're welcome."

"Mom?" Holly bursts through the front door before I can say anything else to Gwen. "How are you feeling? How's your arm? Do you need anything?" She rushes over to my side.

"Breathe," I tell her, laughing. "I'm fine. Just a bit sore. How was school?"

"Boring," Holly sighs and makes herself comfy on the couch cushions.

"How was chemistry?" Gwen asks.

Holly cringes. "Hard. I might need your help this weekend. I have a unit test next week."

"Sure," Gwen replies.

"Thanks." Holly smiles at her.

The rest of the night is surprisingly uneventful. The three of us are able to hang out with light conversation and no fighting or awkwardness. I'm hoping we are all reaching a new level of normalcy and that we can all start to deal with the past in a mature way. Little did I know, this was only the beginning.

TWENTY-THREE
Holly

The week after Mom came home from the hospital, I could tell things were going to be different. I couldn't remember Mom being home this much in years. She didn't even go into her office, or at least she didn't when I was home; maybe she was secretly working away all day while I was at school. But she seemed different; she seemed less distracted and more focused on me. We ate dinner together every night, most nights Gwen ate with us too and Duane even stopped by a few times too. The three of us had somehow avoided the topic of our complex triangle mother-daughter relationship for almost one week.

By the time Friday morning rolled around I was growing antsy. I woke up at four in the morning and stared up at my dark bedroom ceiling. I needed to meet my dad. Ever since I had learned of his existence, learned of his name and that he never knew about me, it was eating at me. I get out of bed and walk into my bathroom. I turn on the shower and let it run for a minute until the water is hot and I begin to see steam. I step into the shower and sit down on the white porcelain floor. I feel the hot water dropping against my skin. I stay that way for a while, until the water turns a lukewarm temperature and my hands feel like wrinkly prunes.

I towel-dry my hair, put on some jeans and a sweater and just before 5am, quietly walk down the hallway to Mom's room. I slowly open her door, trying not to wake her. "You're up early," Mom says, almost the second her door opens.

"I couldn't sleep. You're up early too."

"I miss running." She turns on the lamp on her nightstand and pats the bed beside her. I cross the room, pull up the covers and slip into bed beside her.

"Just a few weeks of rest and you'll be back to it," I say, leaning back into the pillows.

"I know, it's just strange not being able to do something that I'm used to doing every day. So what's up?"

I take a deep breath and before I can even think about them, the words escape my mouth. "I want to go visit him."

Mom sits up a little higher in bed. "Chris?"

"Yes. Will you take me?"

"Yes," she says without hesitation.

"Do you know where he is?" I ask.

"Yes," she says again. "I had someone look into it recently. I wasn't keeping it from you…"

"I know," I cut her off. "There's been a lot going on – I get it."

"He's still in Alder. When do you want to go?"

"Can we go today?" I feel my chest start to tighten a little bit. I know that if I don't do this soon that I'm going to chicken out. Mom nods in response. She lightly touches my arm with her good hand. "Are you okay to drive with your wrist?" She nods again. "What do we tell Aunt Gwen?"

"Whatever you want," she replies. "Give me twenty minutes. Then we can go. We've got a bit of a drive ahead of us." I'd never been to Alder, but I knew it was at least two hours away.

I wait downstairs for Mom and pray that Gwen wouldn't come down and see us getting ready to leave. When Mom comes down to the kitchen, I hand her a buttered bagel and a traveler's mug of coffee.

"Thanks," she says and gives me a kiss on the cheek. "Let's go."

We don't speak for the first half of the drive. Traffic is light and I can tell by the signs we keep passing that we are making good time. I begin to wonder what Alder will look like.

"How come you've never taken me there before?" I ask Mom, while staring out the window.

"Where? To Alder?" Mom laughs. "It's honestly no different than Fife Springs. A little smaller, maybe. There was no reason to go there after your grandparents passed away."

"I wish I had gotten to meet them."

"Me too. They would have loved you."

I don't know what to say to that, so I don't say anything. We drive the rest of the way in silence. An hour and a half later, shortly after 8am, we enter Alder. Mom is right; it is almost exactly like Fife Springs. I can see why it had been so appealing to Mom and Gwen. We drive through the town, which takes less than ten minutes.

Mom shows me their old high school and then turns down Third Street. She drives down it halfway and parks across the street from a classic white colonial-style house. The house has steps leading up from the sidewalk and a path that cuts through the beautifully manicured lawn, leading up to the front door.

"Nice house," I say.

Mom nods in response. "Are you ready?"

I shrug. "Are you going to come with me?"

"Of course," Mom replies. She unbuckles her seat belt and opens the car door. I do the same and walk around the car to meet her. We cross the street and stand on the sidewalk side-by-side, staring up at the house. My feet are frozen. After a minute of standing, Mom gently takes my arm and leads me up the set of four stairs to the path. We walk to the front door, where I stop again, unable to move. I actually can't believe that this is happening – that I'm going to meet my dad. A man that I had wondered about for my entire life. Suddenly, I feel extremely nauseous.

"Do you want me to knock?" Mom asks. I'm about to reply when the front door opens. A man I've never seen before stands there staring at us.

"Katie?" He squints at Mom like he was looking at a Ghost. "Katie Sherwood. You live and breathe."

"Hello Chris," Mom says, formally. "It's been a long time."

"Seventeen years," He says and then he turns to look at me. "Hi," he says. I take in his appearance. He's tall, around 6 feet. He has lightly tanned skin, dirty blonde hair that is slicked back neatly to one side; light brown eyes and I see a line of stubble on his chin. He is exactly the kind of man I would have pictured Gwen with. "Gwen," he says suddenly, looking into my eyes. I don't say anything, but beside me, Mom grabs my hand and squeezes it.

"Chris, this is Holly, my daughter," Mom interjects quickly.

"Sorry," he mutters. "You look just like someone." He turns to look at Mom, "She looks exactly like Gwen."

"I think I'm going to be sick," I say.

Mom stays completely composed, but she wraps her arm around my waist to stable me. "Chris, we need to talk. That's why we're here."

He nods, again staring at me like he has just seen a ghost. "Come in," he takes a step back and opens the door. "My wife, Emilie, should be back soon. She's just dropping the kids off at school." Kids. He has kids.

"You have kids," Mom repeats.

"Three," he leads us into the living room. "Sam is ten, Jenna is eight and Elliot is five." He motions to the wall where I see a family picture. Two brothers and a sister. And a gorgeous woman beside them.

I am too out of it to even look at the rest of the room. I sit down on a nice-looking couch beside Mom, and Chris sits in an armchair across from us.

"I'm sure you're wondering why we are here," Mom says. She speaks clearly and is well-composed as always. I, on the other hand, feel like a complete disaster. I don't know how she does it.

"I'm a little confused," Chris admits. He laughs awkwardly, like he's trying to lighten the mood. I don't know him, but I can tell he's nervous. His face has turned a pink-rose colour, and I can see a light glistening of sweat across his face.

"When I introduced Holly to you as my daughter," Mom begins. "That wasn't entirely true. Yes, Holly is my daughter. I have raised her since she was a baby, but I didn't give birth to her. She's not my biological daughter, she's –."

"Mine," Chris finishes for her. "And Gwen's." His eyes go wide. He runs his right hand through his hair, messing up his perfect looking hair. "Holy shit."

Mom keeps talking. She fills him in on how I had come to be her daughter, what had happened to Gwen, and how Gwen's cancer that had led to everything coming out in the open.

"I can't believe she never told me," he says and sighs. He doesn't sound angry, just hurt. He looks over at me. "I'm so sorry, Holly. If I had known…"

"I know," I choke the words out and swallow hard. My throat feels dry.

Mom and Chris talk for a few more minutes and then Mom says we should go. I am thankful for this, as I'm nowhere near ready to meet his wife and kids. We exchange phone numbers and emails. I notice that Mom gives him Gwen's contact info as well.

"Is it okay if I call you?" he asks me, and then turns to Mom. "Is that okay?" Mom smiles at him reassuringly and nods.

"Yeah," I say, lamely. "That would be nice."

"Okay," he says as we walk to the door together. "I'd like to see you again soon, Holly," he says. "I mean, if that's okay with you."

I nod in response. My mouth is even drier now, and it's really all that I can do.

"Can I give you a hug?" he asks, even more awkwardly. I nod again. He pulls me into his arms and hugs me. His arms feel warm and safe, like Mom's do. I rest my head on his chest for a few seconds and he rests his one hand on my curls. Then he pulls away. "We'll talk soon."

"Sounds good," I say. Mom puts her hand on my back and leads me out the door.

"Thanks, Chris," she says. "We'll be in touch soon." Together, we leave the house walking back down the front steps to the car. I hear the front door close behind us as we walk. We get to the car and I run over to the grass, hunch over and throw up as discretely as possible. I stand up and take a deep breath. "Are you okay?" Mom calls from the other side of the car.

I wipe my mouth, nod and get into the car on the passenger side. Mom gets in on her side. "Are you hungry?" she asks me. She puts her hand on my forehead to feel my temperature. I lean backwards into the seat, away from her hand. I'm not sick.

"Not really," I shrug and buckle up my seatbelt.

"Okay. We can stop for lunch, but not here."

"Why not here?"

"Too many people know me here. This town is the same as it was eighteen years ago," she tells me. "I don't want people to know why I was here. That's not fair to Chris." I nod in agreement.

We drive out of Alder and stop at a diner in the next town over. The diner looks like it opened in 1970 and hasn't changed since then. We slide into a red shiny booth and a waitress named Maggie immediately comes over and takes our drink order. Mom orders a coffee and I ask for a glass of water. Maggie brings us our drinks and I pretend to look at the menu.

"Want to split a BLT on rye and a salad?" Mom asks.

"Sure." I push the menu aside. Mom motions Maggie back over to us and places our order, then she takes both of my hands across the table and looks me directly in the eyes.

"How are you feeling about everything?" she asks me.

I bite my lip, hesitating. "Okay, I guess. He seems really cool, and honestly, I was expecting him to react in a less than positive way."

"Chris has always been calm and collected."

"Kind of like you."

"I have my moments," she smiles at me.

"I'm scared to see Gwen."

"Don't be scared." Mom wrinkles her eyebrows. "I can deal with Gwen, it will be fine. You have the right to meet your dad. Gwen can't stop that from happening."

"Thanks for taking me." My voice is sincere. "I couldn't have done that without you. I know this is probably really weird for you too."

"Just a little." Mom lets out a forced laugh. "They definitely don't write hand books for this kind of thing."

"I really do appreciate it."

"I know, sweetie." Our order comes and we eat quickly before getting back in the car for our drive home.

Finally I ask Mom a question that I've thought about a lot since finding out that Gwen was my biological mom. "Didn't you ever want kids of your own?"

Mom shoulder-checks and aggressively pulls the car over and stops it on the side of road. She turns her whole body towards me and looks me attentively in the eyes. "You're my own," she says fiercely. "You've always been my own. I may not have carried you for nine months or given birth, but besides those two things you have been with me for sixteen years. I was there with you every night when you were colicky and would cry and cry. I was there for your first steps, your first words, your first day of school, your first broken bone. You've been with me since the beginning and I would never think of you as not mine. You've always been enough for me. I never needed anyone else."

"I know, Mom," I smile at her, feeling like I could cry out of gratefulness. "But didn't you ever want more kids? What about Duane, doesn't he want kids?"

"Actually, he doesn't."

"Really?"

She sighs. "He has always been very career-focused, as have I. It's something we had talked about but it wasn't in the cards for us."

"What does that mean?" I'm curious.

Again, she sighs. "I can't have biological kids of my own."

It's amazing how tone of voice can relay so much about a person's emotions. She doesn't look upset when she tells me this; she says it in a way that I can tell she has come to terms with it and that it truly doesn't matter to her.

"I'm sorry," I say, looking down at my hands. I'm not sure what else to say.

"It's okay," she says. "Remember when you were seven and I had my appendix out?"

I nod in response.

"I didn't actually have my appendix out, I had a hysterectomy. I had something called endometrioses and that was what they needed to do to fix it. I had never really thought about having another baby, it had always just been me and you…that just made it official."

"That must have been hard."

"It was fine."

I smile at her nonchalant manner. Leave it to Mom to act like someone taking away her reproductive system wasn't a big deal.

"Mom?" I ask. "Do you think he really wants to see me again?"

"I do." She doesn't even hesitate. "Chris – your dad – he's a good guy, Holly. I haven't seen him since before you were born, but I grew up with him and he's always been a good guy. I can bet that if he had known about you that he would have been in your life from the beginning." Hearing these words brings a rush of anger through my body. She's not even looking at me and she knows this. "I know that probably makes you mad."

I clench my jaw a bit and nod. "I just don't know what's going to happen now. He has a family."

"We'll figure it out," Mom says confidently.

For the millionth time I wonder why Gwen and Mom didn't just tell me the truth years ago and what things would have been like if they had.

We don't talk the rest of the way home and when the house comes into view and Gwen's car is still in the driveway, my hands begin to shake. Mom pulls into the garage and before she even turns off the engine Gwen is standing at the door.

Mom sighs. "This is my battle, not yours," she says, looking me square in the eyes. "I'll deal with her. Don't even worry about it." She unbuckles her seatbelt, opens the door and gets out of the car. I do the same at a much slower pace.

"What the hell did you do, Kate?" Gwen's voice is loud and uncontrolled.

"Inside," Mom says calmly. I watch her rest her hand on the small of Gwen's back and lightly usher her into the house.

"I got a phone call from Chris," she yells. "What were you thinking taking her to go meet him? Are you out of your flipping mind?"

I walk into the kitchen and see Mom standing at the island and Gwen pacing back and forth. I've never seen Gwen like this before.

"Holly wanted to meet her dad," Mom shrugs. My stomach sinks and I know this isn't the right response. Gwen doesn't appreciate feeling under-minded and I know that Mom knows this. They are both angry and hurt.

"That's not your call!" Gwen yells.

"Not my call," Mom says quietly. "Not my call?" She yells just as loudly as Gwen. Then she stops and looks at me. "Holly, can you go to your room for a few minutes please?" She gives me a pleading look like it's not a punishment, but that she is trying to save me. I nod quickly and run up the stairs to my room. I lie down on my bed and can hear them yelling again. They yell for a few more minutes and then it stops. I can't hear what they are saying anymore. I'm suddenly exhausted. I close my eyes and decide to take a quick rest.

A knock on the door jolts me. I slowly sit up and wonder how long I've been asleep for. "Come in," I call. The door opens and I'm surprised to see Gwen, not Mom, standing in the doorway. The look must show on my face.

"Can I still come in?" Gwen asks.

"Yup," I say, feeling my heart rate speed up.

"Sorry about what happened downstairs," Gwen says as she walks over and sits at the end of my bed.

"I just thought if we told you that you'd say no."

"Well, you weren't wrong," Gwen smirks. "I was completely blindsided when Chris called me." I don't say anything and she continues. "He wants to see you again."

"He said that," I frown. "He's married and has three kids."

"I know," she doesn't even look surprised.

"So you knew were he was this whole time?" I'm honestly not the least bit shaken by Gwen's lies anymore.

"I've kept tabs on him over the years," she admits. "I was at a work conference a few years ago and ran into him." A big part of me wants to punch her in the face when she tells me this. I wish she wouldn't have.

"So what, are you going to come with me when I meet him again? Are we going to have some big family reunion?"

She shakes her head. "I'll leave that up to your mom. I don't plan on seeing Chris again." She sounds hurt, almost hostile and while I understand, I don't entirely care either. We sit there staring at each other. I can tell Gwen wants to say something but she doesn't. She just keeps on looking at me.

"What?" I finally say.

"Nothing," she looks down. "I just came up to say sorry, that's all."

"Okay." I'm not even sure what she's apologizing for, or if she even knows. I can't really believe we are back at this place again. Just last week it felt like we'd finally broken through all the crap and things were beginning to go back to normal. The feeling was almost unexplainable – a part of me craved Gwen – a need to feel wanted by her, loved by her and close to her. Here she was sitting right in front of me and I had never felt so far away from her in my entire life. "Well, I guess I'll go back to bed." I don't even know what time it is.

She nods, "Good night." She stands up and walks out of my room, closing the door behind her.

The next day, Gwen moves back to her house. She is gone before Mom and I are up for the day. The next month passes quickly. Mom goes back to work and gets her cast off. I'm working my way through classes and counting down the days until spring break. I haven't talked to Gwen since the day I met Chris – my dad. Chris and I have been emailing back and forth for the past two weeks. Him and his wife have invited Mom and I for lunch one day over the break. I was surprised he extended the invite to Mom, even though there was no way I would have gone without her.

I miss Gwen. Things don't feel the same without her. I know her and Mom have been talking occasionally, but she hasn't reached out to me. I feel hurt by her actions, and I also know that she feels

betrayed by mine – even though I don't really think she has the right
to.

It's the first Monday of spring break and I'm in the grocery
store picking up a few things that Mom has asked me to get for
dinner when I see Gwen in the produce aisle. She is holding an apple
in her right hand and examining it like she's trying to decide whether
or not to perform surgery on it. I freeze with my bag of broccoli,
wondering if I should approach her. She doesn't see me yet, but I
give her a once-over. She looks thin – too thin – and pale. I watch
her eyes scan through the bin of apples and I can see how tired she
is. My stomach does a flip and I know that she's sick again. I turn
away from her, but she sees me and calls my name.

"Holly! Wait!"

I stop and turn around, clutching the broccoli to my chest.
"Hey." My breathing is heavy.

"It's been awhile…" She walks over to me and gives me a
once-over. "You're looking well."

You're looking well? What the hell kind of comment is that?
I stare at her like she's a space alien.

She senses my annoyance. "Can I give you a ride home? I
just got off work, so I have a few more things to grab."

"Fine. Me too." I get the rest of my groceries and she gets
hers. She pays for mine, even though I insist she doesn't have to and
we walk to her BMW together.

There are two ways to get to our house from town; she takes
the long way. Sitting in Gwen's car, I am suddenly hit with a wave
of exhaustion. I'm tired of playing these games. "Why didn't you tell
me you're still sick?"

"I haven't known for very long," she answers immediately.
"Last month my blood work was almost normal, and a few weeks
ago everything changed. They found cancer in my liver."

I close my eyes. I didn't know a lot about cancer, but I knew
enough to know that when it reached your liver it wasn't good.
"Does Mom know?"

"Not yet," Gwen says. She pulls the car into the driveway
and shuts off the engine. "It's progressed pretty quickly. I'm on the
transplant list, but it's not looking too good at this point."

"This is unbelievable," I mutter, staring out the windshield.

"What do you mean?" Gwen sounds hesitant.

"We've just been wasting so much time." I swear loudly expressing my frustration.

"Language," she says, cutting me off.

"Would you just shut up already?" I yell. My own volume catches both her and me by surprise. "You haven't talked to me for a month and now you run into me at the fu – freaking grocery store and tell me you're dying? Are you the most self-centered person in the world?"

She closes her eyes and rests her forehead in her hands. "Yes," she says, finally. "I am. I'm sorry. I don't know how to be a parent."

"Well you were doing a pretty good job of it before you told me you were mine," I pointed out. "I'm not sure why it's so hard for you now."

"You're not wrong. Look Holly, I –."

"I can't keep doing this with you Gwen," I say. "I'm tired of you lying to me. I love you, and I'm sorry you're sick, but I'm done with your lies." I open the door, get out of the car and walk inside the house, ignoring her calling after me.

I lock the door, even though Gwen has a key and could come inside if she wanted to. When Mom shows up half an hour later, I'm sitting at the kitchen island eating chocolate chips out of the bag.

"I thought you wouldn't be home till dinner," I say.

She sits down beside me and gently tugs the family sized bag of chocolate chips towards her. She takes a few out and pops them into her mouth before answering. "A little birdie told me you might need me this afternoon."

"Figures." I take some more chips out of the bag and stuff a few into my mouth.

"How are you feeling?" Mom asks, her eyes filled with concern.

"Bad. Mad. Sad. I don't know," I groan.

"I'm sorry."

"Did you know?"

Mom looks sad. "She told me after she told you."

"So was she just never going to talk to us again and then die?"

Mom flinches at the word "die." "Honestly, Holl – I really don't know where your Aunt Gwen has been at these last few months. I think a lot of this chalks up to unfortunate timing. It's a lot for all of us to deal with."

"I just don't know what to do." I flop forward on the countertop and rest my head on my arms. "I'm so tired of her keeping things from me all the time. I feel like she doesn't care about my feelings at all." Mom rubs my back.

"You may not control all the events that happen to you, but you can decide not to be reduced by them."

"Who said that?" I sit back up.

"Maya Angelou," Mom smiles. "I remember when both my parents died and my sister had been on bender after bender for months, I was feeling frustrated and at my wits' end. Someone shared that quote with me and I have never forgotten it. Don't focus on what you can't control, sweetie. You can't control what Gwen and I kept from you or how she's dealing with everything right now. You can control how it affects you and how you choose to respond to her."

I let her words sink in. "You're right," I tell her. "It's just not easy."

"I know, baby." She puts her arm around me and gives my shoulder a light squeeze. "But if anyone can do it, you can."

"So you think I should talk to her?" I ask.

"Maybe just give her a bit of time. If there's one thing I know about my sister, it's that she always comes around."

I nod. "I'll try." I stand up. "Now that you're home you can help me cook dinner"

Mom laughs and stands up as well. "Done."

The next day Mom leaves work midmorning and drives me to see Chris for lunch. I have taken to just calling him Chris because it seems too much, too intimate to refer to him as "Dad" so soon in our relationship. We drive the 90 minutes to Alder, getting there shortly after noon and are greeted by Chris and his wife Emilie. If you saw Mom, Gwen and Emilie Hawkins standing in a line, you would think that Gwen and Emilie were twins, not Mom and Gwen. The resemblance between them isn't hard to miss. It's obvious that Chris has a type.

Emilie is sweet and welcoming. She gives us both hugs and teaches us how to properly pronounce her name – it's not Emily, but Em-ee-leigh. She gives us a tour of their home and says that I will have to meet the kids soon. They are at her parents' for a few days, which is fine with me because I'm not sure I could handle a step mom and half siblings at the same time.

We sit down at the table and she begins to dish out lunch, which looks like some kind of fancy casserole. Chris passes plates to both of us.

"I hope you like it," she says. "Chris didn't mention if either of you have any allergies."

"We don't," I assure her.

"Thanks, Emilie," Mom smiles at her. "This looks great." I realize that if Gwen were with me instead of Mom that there would probably be a lot more tension in regards to Emilie, but with Mom there is no threat to her at all. The adults make small talk for a few more minutes. I take a few bites of the casserole. It has mushrooms in it, not my favourite, but somehow still manages to taste great. Emilie gives off the vibe that everything she does is amazing, yet still seems humble and genuine. I like her.

After a few minutes, a nervous-looking Chris speaks up. "So Katie," he begins. I'm surprised Mom lets him call her Katie. The only people I've ever heard call her by her childhood nickname are Gwen and sometimes Duane. "I wanted to talk a bit about setting up some regular time to for Holly and I to see each other."

"What did you have in mind?" Mom asks. She looks completely composed and unbothered by his suggestion.

"I was thinking that we could start with dinner every two weeks? I could come out to Fife Springs and we could have dinner, just the two of us. And then if you're up for it Holly, I was wondering if you would like to spend one day a weekend with our family. You could spend the whole weekend if you wanted – and if your mom was okay with it – but I thought it might be best to just start slow."

I look over at Mom who gives me a tiny nod. "I think that sounds good," I say. "I don't know about overnight – but I could do one weekend day a month."

"Fine with me," Mom agrees.

"We can figure something out for weekend transportation too," Chris says. "I don't want to put that all on you."

"We can work something out," Mom says.

"This doesn't need to be formal on our side either," Chris says. He's talking fast and looks even more nervous. "I'm just so thankful that you both reached out. I will take whatever time with

Holly I can get." In other words, he wasn't going to fight Mom for
custody. This meant he wasn't an idiot, because you probably didn't
want to fight a judge for custody of her child.

"Holly is sixteen," Mom tells him. "She is old enough to
decide what steps she wants to take in regards to all of this. I will
support whatever she chooses." Under the table she reaches for my
hand and gives it a small squeeze.

"Thank you, Katie." Chris smiles at both of us. "This means
a lot to me."

"Emilie," Mom smiles. "This is delicious. You'll have to
give me the recipe."

After lunch, we hang out for an hour and then headed back to
Fife Springs. At home Mom heads into her office to respond to some
emails. I am officially bored. Griffin texts me and asks if I want to
hang out. I tell him I'm busy. I hear a knock on the front door. I pop
up from the couch as I hear the door open, wondering if it's Gwen.
My heart sinks a tiny bit when I see Duane.

"Hey, kiddo." Duane flashes me his signature grin, complete
with dimples. "I brought food. You up for helping me cook?"

"Depends on what it is." I peer over at the brown paper bags
in his hands.

"Chicken picatta, risotto and salad."

"I'll do the salad," I laugh. "The rest is all you."

"Deal." He lifts the bags up high and places them on the
island.

Dinner is incredible. Duane hadn't starved as a bachelor that
was for sure. I go upstairs to grab a sweater and when I come back
down, Gwen is standing in the kitchen beside Mom, while Duane is
doing dishes at the sink. No doubt about it, he was a keeper.

"Hey," I say, feeling my anxiety level start to rise. This
feeling of nausea and like my body temperature has spiked ten
degrees in seconds wasn't ever a feeling I wanted to get used to.

"I was wondering if you wanted to hang out for a bit," Gwen
looked like death if death was a person. She was pale, her eyes were
red, and her lips were chapped. She wore a toque on her head and an
oversized sweatshirt.

"Want to go for a walk?" I ask.

"Sitting might be easier." She looks nervous, not agreeing
with my original suggestion.

"Sitting is okay."

"We can go for a walk," Duane says.

"Good plan." Mom gives me a familiar look where she seems to speak at me with her eyes. I recognize it immediately as her reaching out to see if I'm okay with her leaving. I quickly nod in response. "See you guys in a bit," she says. Duane dries his hands on a dishtowel, hangs it on the stove and together they walk over toward the foyer.

"Want to sit?" I motion to the couch. She nods. We walk over to the couch and sit down on opposite ends. She doesn't say anything. I'm not sure what to do. I'm exhausted from the circular conversation and I really don't want it to happen again.

"So how's work been?" I ask. It's a stupid question. She looks surprised, but she answers.

"Good. Today was actually my last day," she frowns and I watch her eyes fill with sadness. "I've loved being a doctor."

"Why did you decide to be a doctor?"

She smiles the smallest smile and takes her time answering. "I suppose it was a way for me to do some good in the world after everything that I messed up. I liked being able to help people. I liked getting to meet new people. From a young age I've always felt compassion towards people going through a hard time."

"You're a very compassionate person," I agree. "I wish I had something like that…something that made me want to be something better."

"You will," she says. "You're young, and you have a long time to get there. Think of everything I went through before I became a doctor. Honestly, looking back, I never would have thought I'd get there now."

"You're strong."

"So are you."

"It's genetic."

She smiles at that. "Want to watch a movie?"

"Only if you pick."

"You're too easy," she gets up and walks over to our trunk filled with old DVDs.

"I'll make some popcorn," I say. I walk over to the kitchen again and start collecting the necessary supplies. "Did you find a movie?" I call over to Gwen. She holds up White Christmas and my heart aches. Every Christmas since Gwen has been around we've watched White Christmas together. I feel a fast wave of emotional pain in my heart because I know exactly why she's picked it for us to watch in the middle of March. We will never have another Christmas together again.

"Classic," I say nonchalantly.

"I thought so too." Gwen smiles a big smile now that reveals some of her pre-cancer self.

Mom and Duane walk in when the popcorn is popping. "Movie night!" Duane exclaims. "Yes! I'll do the drinks."

"White Christmas?" Mom looks at the paused opening movie credits on the TV screen. She gives Gwen a knowing look and sighs heavily. Duane hands her a glass of wine and she immediately takes a sip. He opens up a beer for himself and after a few minutes presents Gwen and I with hot chocolate in Christmas mugs. Did I mention how much I like Duane? We all squish onto the couch together and begin to watch the movie.

Within the first twenty minutes we reach the scene that is so familiar to me, Judy and Betty singing "Sisters" in the club. Mom and Gwen know the song by heart. They also take it upon themselves to belt it out every time that we watch the movie. I saw Gwen's eyes lock with Duane's as she sang the line, "Lord help the mister who comes between me and my sister, and Lord help the sister that comes between me and my man." He winks at her in response.

"That was beautiful, ladies," Duane laughs. "And to think I've missed out on that performance for all these years."

"Hence the making up for lost time," Gwen tells him. A heavy silence fills the room following her comment and no one says anything. We watch the rest of the movie – Mom, Gwen and I snuggled up together. Duane had fallen asleep, so Mom tucks him in with a blanket on the couch. We get Gwen situated in the guest room and then head our separate ways to bed.

After I had changed into my pajamas and was curled up in bed, I couldn't help but think that this had been a night that I would never forget.

TWENTY-FOUR
Kate

I was waiting for the phone call that would change my life. I had spent a lot of my life waiting. Waiting for Gwen to figure her life out after our parents died, waiting for Holly to decide to like me again, waiting for the right job to come along before all of that. It was the beginning of April and I knew that Gwen didn't have much time left. We saw each other daily now; Holly and I would have dinner at her house almost every night. She had a nurse who stayed with her 24 hours a day and it was very clear that at this point they were just making her comfortable.

I wasn't sure what was going to happen when Gwen wasn't there anymore, and honestly I was scared shitless. Yes, Gwen and I had spent the first few years of Holly's life apart, but it hadn't been easy. I had ached for my sister. That was the interesting thing about twins – the connection; it never went away, even when you weren't together. I wondered what would happen when she died. Would I feel like part of me had died? Would it hurt? I had spent the past eight or more years wondering if Holly liked Gwen more like she liked me and if Gwen had made the wrong decision. Would Holly be okay when Gwen was gone? Would she resent me for not telling her our secret sooner? These were the questions that kept me up at night, and the questions that I had no answers to.

I go to work and when I'm not there or with Gwen, I pass the time with Holly and Duane. Duane and I are planning to get married at the end of August, before Holly goes back to school. It will be a small wedding, a civil ceremony and then a restaurant reception with fifty of our closest friends and family. We'd talked about moving the wedding up so that Gwen could be there, but I knew Gwen didn't have the energy for a wedding right now. Duane told me almost daily that we could move the wedding up if I wanted to, but at the end of the day it was also easier for Holly not to have to deal with change and transition while Gwen was in her last days.

The call came on a Tuesday afternoon in the middle of April. Kal, Gwen's nurse, told me that she wasn't doing very well at all.

Her vitals were inconsistent and she had been in and out of consciousness a few times. I'm not sure if it was fate or just coincidence that I didn't have to be in court at all that day. I was working on some paperwork when my phone rang. The second I hung up the phone I grabbed my coat and purse and rushed out of the courthouse.

On my way to my car I call Duane. He answers on the first ring.

"Hey," he sounds groggy. I groan. I'd forgot he had been up most of the night working.

"Sorry," I say immediately. "I can call you later. I forgot you worked all night."

"It's okay," he clears his throat. "What's up?"

"I'm picking up Holly from school. Kal called. They don't think Gwen has much time left."

"I'm sorry to hear that, babe," Duane's voice is hushed and his tone is grief stricken. "Do you want me to come?"

"Give us a bit first."

"Not a problem. How about you let me know when?"

"I will. Thanks for understanding. I love you."

"Love you too."

I hang up my phone, get into my car and drive the quick five-minute distance to the school to get Holly. I feel an unusual sense of franticness as I walk into the school. I'm having a hard time catching my breath, my nerves are jolted and I notice that both my hands are shaking as I reach for the front door of the school. I take two deep breaths and walk inside.

I quickly approach the front office and explain why I am there. I sign Holly out for the day and, a few minutes later, I see her walking towards me.

"Is she dead?"

Her words throw me. I stare at her for too long before replying. I see her eyes fill with sadness, fear and something else. Relief. I frown. I don't have time to wonder about this right now. "No, she's not dead. Sorry, I didn't mean to scare you." I sigh. "She's not doing well though. We need to go." Holly nods. She follows me out of the school.

We drive in silence to Gwen's house. When we get there, we are greeted by Kal who informs us that Gwen is awake. "She seems more chipper and alert," she tells us. I've read enough to know that this can be common for people who are about to die.

"That's good," Holly mumbles. I'm not sure if she is even talking to anyone. She seems distracted.

"Ready to go in?" I say aloud, but not meaning to. I realize that I'm asking myself this, and that I am nowhere near ready. A single tear falls down my cheek. Holly takes my hand, and together, we walk into Gwen's room.

I wonder if Holly is beginning to become accustomed to seeing people in hospital beds. Gwen is lying in a bed that we had moved to her house. She is slightly propped up and her eyes are closed. Her face is a yellow/white; dark circles make her eyes look sunken deep into her face. She looks awful. I hear Holly sniffle beside me, and I watch as she wipes tears off her face. I walk over to Gwen and sit on the bed beside my sister. I take her hand in mine and softly squeeze it.

"I'm here, Gwennie," I whisper, using my childhood nickname for her that she hated.

"Katie," her eyes open. I see her trying to smile, but she can't. "I'm sorry," she whispers. "I'm so sorry."

"Shh," I softly stroke her hair. "It doesn't matter anymore, just rest."

"Thank you for taking care of her," Gwen mumbles. "For always taking care of me. I owe you everything."

"You would have done the same for me," my voice begins to crack. I try to remain composed, but the tears freely begin to flow.

Holly sits down on the other side of Gwen. "Hi," she says.

"Hey, pretty girl." Now Gwen smiles. "I'm glad you made it."

"Me too."

I stand up and move away from the bed to give them some space. They whisper back and forth for a few minutes and then I hear Holly say, "I love you too, Mom." I feel a force as heavy as a brick fall deep into my chest. I keep myself composed, but it's hard to breathe. I understand the gift Holly is giving to Gwen. I understand why. That doesn't mean that it hurts me any less.

Early the next morning, I wake up around three with a sharp pain in my chest again, like someone has just pushed a sharp object into it. I wonder if I'm having another panic attack. I sit up and breathe for a minute and the pain subsides. A strange feeling I've never felt before overcomes me. I feel emptiness deep in my soul and the most sorrow I have ever felt. I lay in bed, waiting.

An hour later my phone rings. I pick it up and listen to Kal tell me that Gwen had stopped breathing just after three in the morning. I hang up the phone and curl myself up into a ball. I feel a multitude of emotions that I don't know how to comprehend: sadness, pain, anxiety, freedom, guilt and even the slightest bit of relief. I don't know how long it is before I get out of bed, but eventually I do. I walk over to the window and see a dark sky, filled with stormy clouds. I shiver.

I pick an oversized cardigan up off of a chair and shrug it on over my shoulders; very quietly I make my way down the hall to Holly's room. Like a mouse, I push open the door as slowly as possible, trying not to wake her. I see the silhouette of Holly sitting up in her bed in the dark room. The streetlight shines through the half open blinds outlining her still figure. I pause and take a deep breath.

"Are you awake?" I whisper. The nightstand light flips on in response.

"You scared me," Holly breathes. She has her hand placed over her chest.

"Sorry." I bite my top lip in hesitation and then cross the room to her bed, snuggling in beside her.

"It's four in the morning," Holly informs me. I don't say anything. I'm rarely at a loss for words, but with all my heart I don't want to deliver this news to her.

"Kal called me a while ago," I start and stop because I really can't say what I need to say next.

"She's gone," Holly finishes for me and it's not a question, but a statement.

"I'm so sorry." I intertwine my hands together on my lap and squeeze them tightly.

"Me too." Holly puts her head on my shoulder. I close my eyes and try to forget about the list of things I need to do that is already compiling in my head. I take another deep breath, and with this one, the tears begin to fall. I feel my body begin to shake.

"Mom?" Holly pulls back and looks at me.

"I just can't believe she's gone," I sniffle.

"I know." Holly is much more composed than me. " It's going to be okay."

I push my head back against the headboard of her bed. "When did you become the strong, composed one?"

"I have a good role model," Holly winks. "Honestly, Mom. I said my goodbyes to Gwen, I knew it was coming. Everything has been so crazy, I feel kind of..." She let her voice trail off.

"Relieved?" I wince, feeling like I shouldn't share such an intimate feeling.

"Yeah." Holly looks concerned. "I'm sorry, I know..."

"Don't be sorry," I cut her off. "I get it." I pull her in close to me. "I love you so much, Holl. I hope you know that."

"I do. I love you too, Mom."

We stay like that, her in my arms, for a long time, not speaking, but breathing together. I listen to our breathing soft and slow and synchronized. Losing Gwen is going to be one of the hardest things we've ever had to go through, but I know that having Holly by my side is going to make it that much easier.

TWENTY-FIVE
Holly

Some days are harder than others. In the first few weeks there is so much to do. We go through Gwen's apartment, we decide what to keep and what to donate. Then we arrange a memorial service. People bring food, and lots of it. It's so nice of people to think of us and I know that Mom appreciates it, but I'm getting to the point where I think my stomach is going to implode if I eat another casserole.

I'm having trouble sleeping. The day after Gwen's memorial is a Sunday. In the middle of the night I sneak into the guestroom where Gwen had slept so that I can feel close to her. I see Gwen everywhere. Her ghost lingers throughout our entire house and no matter where I look, I'm filled with memories of her, memories of us, memories from before I knew the truth about her and memories after I did.

I remember the last conversation we had together. She told me she was proud of me. She told me not to worry. She told me how much she loved me. She told me how sorry she was for everything. I could almost feel the pain she felt as she whispered to me, "I love you, my baby." My hands shook as I whispered my final words to her, "I love you too, Mom." My arm was on her wrist and I felt her pulse speed up. Her eyes filled with tears, a reflection of my own. I kissed her one last time before I left her.

As soon as I walked away from her, I felt the weight lift off my chest. The pressure was gone; the need to balance both of them between me would no longer exist. Although I felt relief, I missed Gwen more than I had ever missed anyone in my life. There was now a hole in my heart that I wasn't sure would ever go away. Before everything had happened, Gwen had been the best aunt I could have imagined. She had been a friend, someone I could confide in, like a sister to me. Sometimes I wish that they'd never told me the truth, because if they hadn't maybe I wouldn't be stuck feeling like a piece of me was always missing.

With Gwen dying, Mom and I were still we, although far

more weathered and much less complicated. Soon things would change again when Duane became her husband, and then things would probably change again as I continued to get to know Chris and his family. I knew that would be hard, but Mom had told me many times how Duane, and even Chris, weren't taking away anything from our family, but adding to it.

I sigh and curl up into the fetal position on Gwen's old bed. I take a pillow – her old pillow – and hold it tightly to my body. It still smells like her, like fresh spring morning dew. I stay there like this until sleep comes, feeling the warm comfort and security of all of Gwen's old ghosts surrounding me, knowing that even though she is gone I'll always have a piece of her somewhere.

Acknowledgement

Well, this book has been a long time coming. Thank you to everyone who helped make this project possible. To Holly and Elya, for reading and re-reading and patiently waiting for me to finish. To Todd, for your encouragement in this project, as well your superb editing skills. To Logan, for bringing my vision of the cover to life and for changing it many times when I wanted to see it a million different ways.

To my babies, Felicity, Dax and Brynn. For playing nicely when I was in the writing zone (most of the time). To Joel, for always encouraging me to write, giving me time to write and being mostly patient with me when I'm writing in my head and ignoring you! I love you!

To my mom, for being my number one cheerleader. To all of my family and friends who have encouraged me to write and helped me get this far.

About The Author

Vanessa Johnson

Vanessa Johnson was born and raised
in Vancouver, British Columbia,
where she still resides today.
In her spare time, she enjoys reading,
serving in her community and
spending time exploring outside
with her family. Twisted Roots is her second novel.

Books By This Author

A Candle in the Wind (Vanessa Orivolo)

17-year-old Aria Brooks just moved to a new town with the weight of the world on her shoulders. Dealing with the recent death of her father while struggling to befriend her new step-father, nothing seems to be going her way. Then Aria meets Matt Lawson, who is unlike anyone she has ever met before, and the angry girl who was afraid to trust slowly starts to let him in.

Aria and Matt soon become inseparable as he helps her unearth buried emotions surrounding her father's death and slowly start to trust the people around her. But will Aria be able to persevere when tragedy strikes a second time, or will she close herself off from the world for good?

Manufactured by Amazon.ca
Bolton, ON